SEAL CHILD

SEAL CHILD

SYLVIA PECK

DRAWINGS BY

ROBERT ANDREW PARKER

MORROW JUNIOR BOOKS / NEW YORK

Printed in the United States of America.
1 2 3 4 5 6 7 8 9 10
Library of Congress Cataloging-in-Publication Data
Peck, Sylvia.
Seal child/Sylvia Peck; drawings by Robert Andrew Parker.
p.   cm.
Summary: While entranced by the seals that swim off the shore of
the Maine island she visits during holidays, sixth grader Molly
befriends an interesting girl her age who seems different from other
humans.
ISBN 0-688-08682-9
[1. Seals (Animals)—Fiction. 2. Supernatural—Fiction.
3. Friendship—Fiction. 4. Maine—Fiction.] I. Parker. Robert
Andrew, ill. II. Title.
PZ7.P3395Se   1989
[Fic]—dc20   89-33700   CIP   AC

For Sage and for Ouzo

Ruby's Song

CHAPTER ONE

This wasn't like waking up in my own room. This was better. This was Maine. Ambrose Island. I snuck one hand out from under the covers and touched the windowpane for one second. *Cold*. You could even feel the cold seep in at the bottom edge. I shivered and snuggled deeper under my quilt. Everything was perfect: Mom and Dad down the hall, me in my bed, and Douglas, my little brother, still asleep just across from me. I liked having my bed near the window. I traced my name, *Molly Bryson,* and then, *Molly Jane Bryson,* but it didn't show because of the frost. Everything was the same as the summer before, except that it was so

1

cold. I scratched a little space out with my fingernail, and then a bigger one to be able to see the ocean. Hello, ocean.

Douglas was twisting around in his covers. He's only three. Half of him was uncovered. He had his blue flannel Superman pajamas on, the ones with the feet. He twisted around some more and rubbed his eyes. Great. Not even one second of privacy. In our regular house, back in Boston, I had my own room. In Boston, Douglas would be way down the hall, on the other side of the bathroom, not squeezed in with me.

"Moll—" Douglas began. He can't say Molly yet; he just says Moll. *Moll*. I hate it. It sounds like the name of a cow.

"I'm *sleeping*, Douglas." I rolled on my side, with my back to him and all the covers pulled up. No privacy at all. One tiny oak chest between us. On top of the chest, a huge white bowl and pitcher, which is how they used to wash up before they had regular sinks in the bathrooms. My mom likes things like that, for decoration.

"*Moll*." More Douglas, and louder. Now Clyde was awake, too, wagging his tail and thumping against the side of my bed. I ignored Douglas and reached down to pet Clyde. Clyde is all black and glossy and has the softest, silkiest fur for a Labrador. Dad says he's only part Labrador, but that only makes him smarter.

"Honey, can you see what Douglas wants?" Mom's voice was muffled, coming from their room. Oh, great. Now Mom was up.

"He doesn't want anything, Mom," I yelled. "He's fine."

"*Juice*," shrieked Douglas. Noise is one of his favorite things.

"Can you get that for him, hon?" Mom asked.

"Okay," I yelled. I got out of bed really fast because the wood floor was so cold. I grabbed my sweat shirt.

"Make sure you wear slippers," called Mom.

"Okay," I yelled again. I hate slippers.

Douglas followed me to the refrigerator. So did Clyde. I pulled the cellophane off one of those cranberry-juice boxes. I even had the straw poked in for Douglas when I handed it to him.

"Okay, Douglas, now take this back to your bed."

He shook his head.

"Take it in with Mom and Dad, then." He shook his head again. Boy, anything can be a game with him.

I opened the cupboard and got out the box of Milk-Bones for Clyde. I gave him three. He gulped them down so fast, he left gritty pieces all over the floor, and he wouldn't lick them up, even when I pointed. I tried not to step on that part of the floor. "Don't slobber, Clyde," I said, but he just sat there drooling, so I gave him one more Milk-Bone, which he cracked in half on the first bite. Douglas grabbed for the other half.

"Douglas, don't EAT that!" I said, and he started to cry, so I picked him up and took him in to Mom.

Dad pulled the pillow over his head. "Nice try, Dad," I said. No way was he going to be able to sleep.

"What happened, Douglas?" crooned Mom.

"Nothing happened," I said.

"Shhhhhh," said Dad.

"Did Molly yell at you?" asked Mom, coaxing him to talk. Douglas nodded, and he looked at me as if I'd just done the worst thing in the world.

"But he was going to eat Clyde's Milk-Bones," I said.

Dad groaned. "Is it too much to ask for a little peace and quiet around here?" he asked. Then he grinned. That meant he was on my side. At least we both knew how stupid it was to be so noisy.

"Shh, Dougie, Molly didn't mean it," Mom said. I rolled my eyes. "What would make it better?" she asked, wiping the tears off his face. She was always

4

talking to Douglas that way, like they were a team.

"*Juice*," said Douglas. He'd just about stopped crying, but when he started shouting for juice, it didn't look good.

"I'll get his juice," I said, and I stamped back into the kitchen for his cranberry carton and took it back. By then, Mom had him tucked in under the covers, between her and Dad.

"What do we have here?" said Dad. "Is it . . . can it be . . . Superman?" Douglas loves to play Superman. He forgot all about his dumb juice. Dad let him walk all over the bed, in his Superman flannels with a cape made out of a pillowcase. Then Douglas started bouncing on Dad's stomach, and I ran back to get dressed.

Clyde was so excited, he jumped up on my bed and flopped down on top of me while I put on my socks. Clyde doesn't understand what it means to lie down *next* to someone. He starts by sitting directly on the person. That's how he knows where to lie down: wherever you are.

I checked my pockets to see if I had any money. There's a neat General Store, about two blocks away, that opens every morning early for the fishermen. They sell everything you can think of, including hot chocolate and butterscotch sticks. Clyde opened his eyes

5

while I checked, and then closed them again. Dad says Clyde watches over our family as if we were his flock of sheep.

Just then Clyde gave out a long trembly sigh. It means *home*.

"But we're not home, Clyde," I whispered against his thick glossy neck, "we're on Ambrose!" and I threw my arms around him and hugged him to me, even though, by the ocean, he tends to have this old fish smell.

"You old fishy breath," I said, and really squeezed. I must have squeezed too hard, because all of a sudden Clyde scrambled free. He hates it when I talk about his breath. I have to disguise myself so he is fooled by my voice. "Sweet, sweet, smelly," I say, and pet his silky ears. It always works. You touch his ears and he's completely off guard. He'll close his eyes and lean against you. Sometimes I think he looks like a glossy black seal, his ears lie so flat and still when he's happy.

CHAPTER TWO

"Come on, Clyde," I yelled, and banged out the front door. Everything looked beautiful when I got outside. The trees were hung with icicles. I didn't remember them from the night before when we'd bundled in. All I remembered was the ferry ride to the island: how Dad took me outside, and we held on to the railing and watched for the first lights of the island. It began to snow as we watched and the flakes were large and white before they melted away against the dark water.

Safe on land now! I giggled and jumped backward into a snowbank. I heard Mom call to me from the cottage and ask if I was warm enough. "Yes," I said,

still giggling. Clyde kept trying to lick at my face. He loves it when you're down at his same height. I batted snow at him and he sneezed.

"Don't be long, honey, I'm making French toast," called Mom.

"Okay."

I started running off toward the top of the bluff.

"Why don't you stop by Ruby's?" she called out. Ruby is our neighbor, only she lives on Ambrose year round, and we only visit.

"I will," I yelled. It was starting to snow already. Big fluffy flakes.

"Molly, wait a second! Why don't you invite Ruby for breakfast?"

I put out my tongue to catch some snow.

"Okay?" called Mom.

I shouted back, "Okay." Clyde was already half-way down the road. I grabbed his collar so he wouldn't take the path down to the shore.

"C'mon, Clyde, we're going to Ruby's," I said. I started to run toward her cottage so he'd follow me. You don't need a leash on the island. Not like Boston. At home I have to keep Clyde leashed until we get to the park, and he hates it. He's always straining against his collar and making these big gasps. He can pull me right over if I don't watch out, so when he starts running on the leash, I pretend he's my team of horses. We never fall that way.

I knocked on Ruby's door. It was one of those doors with a window, and she had a little curtain fixed at the top of it. I'm so glad we're here, I thought. We'd never come up for winter vacation before. We only visited Maine in the summers, when Dad didn't have to teach college. My dad teaches zoology. Anything animal is okay with him. My mom had the idea to visit Ambrose off-season. "Don't you want to see the birds in winter?" she'd asked. Mom loves birds. "Don't you want to see Ruby?"

I knocked again, my secret knock. One loud, two soft, one loud. Ruby came to the door slowly. I looked around at all the snow and found a stick to throw for Clyde. He looked so sweet jumping through the huge drifts, his coat all sleek and black. Mom was right. She said there'd be more snow on the island than in Boston. On Ambrose, there was so much snow, we could make a whole family of snowmen. In Boston, you'd be lucky to scrape together enough for one snowball.

Just then the door opened.

"Hi, Ruby, it's me." I gave her a big hug, and ran in along with Clyde, and told her all about the drive north, and taking the ferry, and Dad making a fire in the potbellied stove when we first arrived. Ruby is about the oldest person I know. Most of her hair is white, but there are other colors, too. She calls them gray but I call them silver. You know how a horse can have a white mane, but if you look closely, there are lots of different shades of silver? Well, that's what Ruby's hair is like.

She gave me a big kiss and rubbed my face to warm up my cheeks.

"You're invited for breakfast, Ruby."

"Oh, isn't that some treat," she said. "That will be wonderful."

She showed me the sweater she'd been knitting. It was beautiful. It had three different colors of yarn, and white snowflakes knit into the colors. I told her how beautiful it was and she said she'd made it for her granddaughter. I knew she meant me.

I made a face at her.

"Ruby, you know I'm not your granddaughter." I couldn't remember my real grandparents. Douglas never even met them.

"How about my adopted granddaughter? Can you be my adopted granddaughter?"

"Yes." I smiled. "I can be your *adopted* granddaughter."

"How're your mom and dad?"

11

"Fine." I fingered the wool of the sweater.

"And Douglas?"

"Okay," I said, "except when he follows." I started to fiddle with the cord of my sweat shirt. "Douglas copies, plus he makes a mess of the sand." I tried to explain: "He *spoils* things, like when I'm looking for shells."

"How does he spoil things?"

"You *know*." Ruby shook her head. "Well, Douglas isn't careful. Once I tell him I'm finding shells, he'll keep bringing me stones. Even if I tell him, 'only the pretty ones, Douglas,' he'll bring back stupid gray stones about the size of his fist. He doesn't understand at all."

"Maybe he hasn't had as much practice as you've had," said Ruby.

"But he acts as if someone made the whole *world* up just for him," I said. "Whenever he learns a new word, he runs around like a little fire engine, *shouting* it." Ruby laughed.

"It's not funny," I said.

"Oh, yes, it is," she said, and she kept chuckling as she reached for her coat.

I helped her on with her boots. She didn't understand, not about Douglas. The ocean is just about the last place you'd want him. At low tide the beach stretches out so far, the sand dries in ripple marks from the surf. You feel the ridges right through your sneakers. It's like walking over the floor of the ocean, only you never see anyone, only clumps of seaweed and stranded shells. Sometimes you just want to stare and stare, the ocean is so blue, and you wouldn't want anyone there, making all sorts of noise, or heaping up stupid gray stones.

That night when I couldn't fall asleep, Mom came over to tuck me in. She can always tell when I'm not sleepy.

"Mom—" I said.

"Shhh, let's whisper," she said, looking over at Douglas.

"I can't *sleep*," I whispered.

"That's because you're too excited to fall asleep," she whispered back, and smoothed my bangs. I hated that right off.

"I am not too excited," I said. It was the sort of thing she'd say to Douglas. You could say that to Douglas and it would probably be true. You couldn't say it to me.

"What's the matter, honey?"

"Nothing." With my mom, it didn't matter if I said "nothing"—because I always said that. She'd still wait, just in case. I could have told her about school and everybody thinking I was stuck-up, or too young, or how they all seemed to think I knew too much or not enough. But I didn't want to. I liked having secrets. And, as far as my mom and dad knew—nothing was wrong. They were *proud* of me for skipping fifth grade.

"Well," I said, after a pretty long pause, "I can't think of anything to dream about."

Now, you can't blame my mom, but she didn't understand at all. She said horrible boring things like—dream about the seashore and a picnic lunch and seeing Ruby again. I let her finish tucking me in and I kissed her good night and Dad, too, when he came in, but I couldn't believe that she didn't understand. You could say those things to Douglas about the seashore and the picnic, but not to me. I stared out the window and tried not to feel this big disappointment about everything.

I was really the opposite of Douglas, because he was never disappointed, unless something broke, or he fell.

C H A P T E R THREE

C H A P T E R THREE

Dad woke me up early the next morning. He said he had something to show me, so I got dressed in a hurry. Douglas and Mom were still sleeping.

"No," Dad said. "Leave Clyde this time."

"Why?" I asked.

"You'll see." I guessed he'd been up for a while because he was wearing his country clothes—a scratchy wool shirt and thick work boots Mom makes him leave at the door. Good thing she was asleep.

"Hurry," he said, and he held my hand down the path to the beach. The cottages all sit on a bluff and we had to scramble down the path to the sand and rocks below. There are stone steps built for the climb down, but you have to walk a long way to get to them. The path was the shortcut and we always used it. It was fine except for this one tricky part where you had to snake your way around the turn by holding on to an old stump. It was fun. We even did it barefoot in the summer.

I could see the rocks curve out a long way from the far side of the beach. In the summer they get covered with a soft slippery moss from being under-water at high tide. I'd never seen them in winter be-fore—they looked so cold and empty.

"Look," Dad said, and I squinted to see better. The wind was so cold it raised tears. All I could see was the gray of the rocks and the dark of the barnacles.

"When you look at the rocks, at first you'll see nothing." He stood behind me blocking the wind from my back, and he bent to my ear to whisper: "You will think there are no seals"—I smiled because now I knew what I was looking for—"but the seals are there . . . look!" And all of a sudden a huge gray seal raised its head from the closest rock. His hide had that same scarred look the rock had, and—except for the shift of his head—he could have been part of the rock.

"He's very old," Dad said. "Look at the size of him. He must be six feet long."

"How do you know he's old?"

"Look at his eyes," Dad said. I squinted to see.

"You can't see his eyes from here," I said, and Dad laughed. He likes to tease people.

"Why are they here?" I asked. I'd never seen seals in the summer.

"It's low tide . . . they have the place to themselves. At high tide there'd be nothing but cormorants and gulls. The seals breed near here, I think. This time of year they'll pull themselves out of the water if they think they're alone, and lie in the sun."

"It's freezing," I said, though the sun was bright for winter.

"Freezing to you," he said, so we huddled together on the bright windy beach.

"Isn't it cold for them?" I asked.

"No," he said, "they're marvelous creatures for keeping warm." Then he went into this long explanation about heat exchange, which I didn't understand, and how seals have a special layer of fat to protect them from feeling the cold. It made me shiver to think of being in that water, all the same.

Just then the big gray seal pushed off the rock

17

into the ocean and he was gone, and one by one the others pushed off—there must have been five in all. It was only when they moved that I could separate them from the gray rocks they lay on. Then it was only the two of us on the beach and the gulls overhead and the foam of the surf marking the sand.

"Look." Dad pointed out at the water, and there in the bay I could just barely make out a small gray head, and then another, and another, popping up like periscopes. I'd see one, and then another, and by the time I'd look back for the first, she'd have sunk without a sound, and another would surface. From so far away, I couldn't tell which was which or how many were playing. I didn't dare move; it was so special and secret to be watched like that. We stood for a long time to see them rise and stare, and disappear and rise again, soundless, in another place.

C H A P T E R   FOUR

C H A P T E R   FOUR

That afternoon when I went to visit Ruby, I asked her about the seals. She knew about them right away.

"They're always here," she said, joining me on the couch, "the great gray seals." She was wearing her same cable sweater that I remembered from last summer, and the plaid of her housedress showed underneath.

"They look like they're asleep on those rocks," she said, "but they'll sense you coming. Sometimes they'll see you; sometimes they'll smell the human scent on you, and one among them will be the first to slip under the waves, with the others following after.

19

Then he'll be gone and the others, gone too, and you'll think to yourself afterward you saw nothing but rock."

"Where do they live?" I asked. There was a fire going in the fireplace and it made things better, but I was still cold. I was always cold. I sat on her couch and slipped my toes over by her to keep them warm.

"In the caves, out beyond the point, where the surf whittles out the high cliffs." She tucked the afghan around my feet. Her fingers were a little knobby because she was so old, but they always did exactly the right thing.

"Sometimes at night, if you walk out alone and the wind is behind you, you'll hear them. . . . Oh, such a moaning sound will weave round those cliffs. You'd like to pretend it was nothing more than wind and scrub oak, but it's the seals singing of their own, all the same."

"Ruby, you're scaring me," I said, as though it was a ghost story.

She patted my feet under the afghan. "It's not to scare you. They'd never hurt you, the seals. Oh, when I was young, you could wait for them on a warm winter day and see dozens of seals below the cliffs, gathered at the mouth of the caves like children out of school." She smiled at the memory.

"Will you show me where to wait?" I thought how

you could never tell this to Douglas. He'd lose too many words and forget there was a reason to listen.

"If it was a place, I would show you," she said, "but nothing is the same as it was when I was young, not even the seals. They'll not gather where they can be seen. If you walk out to the high bluff, you may see one or two in the moonlight, if you wait. But you must believe in the long watch. One or two is the most you will see."

"We saw five today," I told her, though I should have known better than to contradict her.

"You were lucky," she said, and she clipped her words off sharply. I watched her fingers smooth at the edge of the afghan, where the yarn had frayed.

I got quiet then because I didn't like to think of it as luck. You could call everything luck, if you wanted—bad luck as well as good. That meant the whole stupid fall at school was just my *luck*, and it made me cross to have no one to blame it on.

"Do you know what I thought of when I first saw you?" Ruby asked. I let myself snuggle against her just a little. Her apron smelled like Ivory soap and it was still damp in places.

"I thought to myself how beautiful you were. You can't have been more than four years old. You were wearing an old T-shirt of your father's, and it fit over you like a dress. You were barefoot, and the sand was all crusted up and over your feet and bare calves. You had such a wild look to you, with your hair all tangled and your arms brown from the sun. Your fists were full—both of them. When your father told you who I was, you walked over to the chair I was sitting in and held your hands out to show me what it was you held. But it was sand—nothing more than handfuls of sand. When you opened your fists, the sand slid to the ground. You were so disappointed."

"Well, what do you expect?" I said. "I was only four." I kicked at the bottom of the sofa. This was stupid.

"You don't remember?"

"I guess not," I said.

"Well, you were." She smiled again. "You were very disappointed. And very beautiful."

"I'm not beautiful," I said.

"Hush, Molly, what makes you think we ever know how beautiful we are? No one knows."

"Not true," I said, struggling to sit up so I could make my point better. "Clyde knows how beautiful he is."

I flopped back down.

"Clyde is a dog," she said.

22

"I know that," I said. I thought for a minute. "Douglas knows, too."

Ruby smiled. I guess she was thinking of Douglas then. I thought about Douglas, too, how sweet he looks when he's sleeping, how he doesn't even wake up when Mom lets me go in to give him a kiss good night.

"Tell me another story," I said.

Ruby let out a mock sigh, but I knew she wasn't bothered. She loves to tell stories. I helped her plump up the sofa cushions behind us as the sky turned pink with sunset. You couldn't see the sun set from Ruby's windows because of the hill, but you could watch the sky change colors.

"Once upon a time," she began, "I had a little seal. . . ."

I gave her a look.

"I'm not a baby," I said.

"No, you're not a baby," she agreed. "But once upon a time," she went on softly, "I really *did* have a little seal." She smiled at me then and the way she smiled made me not care if the story was true or not.

"This seal was friendly, like a dog. He'd follow my boat when I'd row the dory out to take lunch to my father and the other fishermen. I never could manage to lose him. Just when I thought I had, he'd rise out of the waves with those laughing eyes. He wore the flat of his belly away climbing up the road to the house to wait for me, then back to the sea each morning and up to the house and back again, day after day. He was so faithful. One afternoon I rowed out five miles so the deep tide would carry him away, and still he lay on my doorstep the very next morning. People began to talk—it was so queer, and my mother kept me in and away from the sea for a month. After that, he stayed with his own, and I couldn't be sure I ever really saw him again. But often, when I rowed out to the men, there'd be this seal swimming close by, and I thought I saw tears in its eyes, and sometimes, on my doorstep in a little pool of brine, there'd be sea lilies, and once a piece of coral in the shape of a ring."

"Do the seals cry, then?" I asked in a sleepy voice. She snuggled me in closer and I let myself be rocked.

"The eyes of the seal are the same as a man's eyes. The cry of the seal is a human cry." It gave me a shiver the way she talked. "Those new seal babies crying in the autumn night, you won't hear any difference between the sound they make and the sound of a real baby."

For a second, I felt as if I couldn't breathe, as

though if she said even one more word, I wouldn't be able to breathe.

"I've seen them cry, and I've seen their tears, though some say it's only seawater. You don't want to see one cry, though. It would break your heart to look into those eyes. It's the eyes of a person that look back at you."

CHAPTER FIVE

CHAPTER FIVE

That night and the next, I snuck out with Clyde after supper and stood on the high bluff to watch for seals. Ruby said to watch for them by moonlight. But it snowed for almost those whole two days, and I couldn't see anything when I went to look. No moon or stars or *anything*. The waves lapped so darkly, I could hear them better than I could see them.

The second night, I stopped at Ruby's on my way home. I stomped in and shook off the snow from my jacket. It made a little ice shelf on my shoulders, and my hair was all soppy. I tried to scrape the snow off Clyde, but he didn't hold still for long.

26

"Look at you!" Ruby said as she hung up my things. She brought me a towel for my hair and another one for Clyde. He hated it.

"No hat?" she asked.

"Oh, Ruby, hats are stupid," I said.

"Stupid?"

"They make you look stupid." She gave me a funny look. "Well, they *do*," I said. "Especially if you have bangs. Hats don't look good on people who have bangs." I pushed at my bangs so they would dry the right way. "It's not good to plaster them down with a hat," I said.

"Such a lot to remember."

"Nobody wears hats," I told her. "None of the sixth graders, anyway. Just the baby grades."

"I see," she said.

Ruby has two windows with lace curtains, one on either side of the fireplace. I went over by one window and straightened out my bangs again. My hair gets a little wavy, especially by the ocean. I frowned, staring at myself in the window. Probably if you saw me, you'd say I had one of those round faces, the kind nobody wants because oval is better. Every night I wished for cheekbones. Mom says I have them, but when she says that, she just means that I have them in the way everyone does. She doesn't mean I

27

have them in a pretty way you could notice.

"Well, Clyde and I didn't see any," I said.

"Any what?"

"*Seals*."

"Patience, Molly," she said, and she picked up her knitting. "It takes patience," she repeated softly.

I looked around the room. The sitting room is my favorite—there's a huge braided rug on the floor, and a couch that you can put your feet on.

"It's not just Molly, it's Molly *Jane*," I said, bouncing a little on my cushion, "and anyway, how long am I supposed to wait for the seals?"

"Not so many questions." She smiled.

"But why moonlight?"

"Isn't it enough that I tell you where to stand and watch?"

"But, Ruby, it's colder at night."

"Of course, it's colder at night."

"And I can't wait out there that long," I said. "I'll get frostbite."

"Surely that's an exaggeration," she said.

"Well, my *ears*," I said, testing them with my fingers. "My ears get so cold, I can't feel them. That's what happens first. First you can't feel them, and next they drop off."

"Couldn't you feel them better if you wore a hat?" she asked.

"Very funny."

"And where did you learn so much about frostbite?" Her needles were clicking.

"From Jeremy Rollins. Jeremy Rollins went skiing last winter with his parents and got frostbite on his big toe."

"And who is Jeremy Rollins?"

"Nobody. Just this sixth grader."

"And did his big toe fall off?"

"No," I said, "but his toenail did. It *did*, Ruby. He showed a whole bunch of us." My face turned hot.

"Well, perhaps if you thought about Jeremy Rollins, your ears would stay warm."

"*Ruby!*"

She chuckled. "Well, it was just a thought. Bundle up those ears and you won't get frostbite." She paused to count her stitches. "But you might have to wait a long time."

"How long?"

"I can't tell you that. They're so shy now—they don't come ashore as much."

"Why not?"

"I'll go make us tea," she said, changing the subject.

Once she left, I stretched out. I took up almost
the whole couch lying down. I could hear her fill the
kettle up and set it on the stove. She asked me a bunch
of questions from the kitchen while she moved around,
getting things ready. All about school, and how I liked
my new teachers, and what it felt like to have skipped
a whole grade.

I got bored by myself, so I went in and sat at the
kitchen table.

"I can't see as well at night," I said.

"Perhaps you weren't meant to," she said. My
stomach rumbled.

"Are there cookies?" I asked. She motioned toward the cookie jar.

I heaped some molasses cookies onto a plate for
us and watched her lift the kettle off the burner.
"That's a big kettle," I said.

"Ought to be," she said. "Three or four of them
will fill a tub."

"A bathtub?"

"No"—she smiled—"an old washtub. It's what
the fishermen soaked their feet in to take the chill out
after a day with the nets."

"Just for feet, then?" I asked, wriggling my toes
and pointing them straight out in front of me.

30

"Not always." She asked me to get the tea canister from the second shelf. I stood on a chair.

"Sugar, too," she said, so I handed her the sack of sugar and the tea canister, and jumped down. Clyde came running in when he heard the cupboards slam.

"What else did they use the tubs for?" I asked.

"For their hands and arms. But that's no story to be telling." I followed her back to the sitting room. Ruby poured out the tea and we each added sugar and milk. I had a cookie right off. Clyde lay back down by the fire and watched the cookies carefully.

"C'mon, Ruby," I said. "Tell."

She hesitated.

"*Please*."

She drank slowly from her cup. I took little sips from mine, too, and waited.

"The fishermen would wash up in them after the day's work," she began. "I watched my own father use one to rinse out the brine and rid himself of the stink and the blood."

"What blood?" I took a big gulp of tea.

"Fish blood," she said.

"Ulch, fish blood." Clyde's tail began to thump against the braided rug. I told him to stay so he wouldn't make me spill.

31

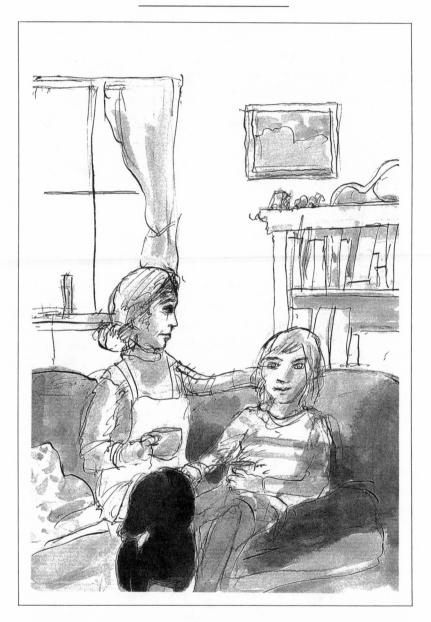

"You eat fish, don't you?"

I nodded.

"Well, when you eat them, they don't have heads, do they? Or scales? Or even bones?"

"Some have bones," I said. "I hate bones."

"Well," she said, "you can't clean fish without getting blood under your fingernails. So my father had to scrub. After a good day's haul, there'd be forty, fifty fish heads out behind the shack. My mother wore herself out washing my father's leggings, and his shirts, and aprons, too—all by hand."

I couldn't finish my cookie.

"Such cold water, too, she'd use," said Ruby. "Afterward, her hands were white as bone. You need cold water for a stain like blood."

"Ulch, blood," I said again, but Ruby kept talking.

"Cull season, she'd strip the clothes off him and burn them, they were so soaked through." She shook her head. "You've never seen such blood."

"What's a cull?" I asked.

"A hunt," she said after a long pause. "All the men went, once a year, at whelping season. They stayed two days, maybe three, out on the far islands."

"What did they hunt?" I almost knew before she answered.

"Seals."

"But they don't hunt them now?" I asked. "Not anymore, right?"

"Not on Ambrose," she said.

CHAPTER SIX

CHAPTER SIX

The next morning, like magic, the sky was bright blue and I was happy because I knew the sky would be clear that night and there would be moonlight to see by.

Mom and I stood by the back porch to watch the birds arrive. In the sunlight, Mom's hair has red highlights, even though it's light brown, like Dad's and mine. Douglas is the only one who's blond. Mom had her coat on, and she opened it up and put her arms around me so the coat was around us both. The floor was so cold, I took turns standing on one foot at a time. Even *with* slippers.

35

I had this idea about Mom and her birdseed, that it was like tending a garden. Every morning she'd sprinkle birdseed on the back porch. And every morning when the birds arrived to feed, Mom would be looking out the window at the colors of their wings. The birds were the only bright colors around; everything else was white or gray.

Now the blue jays were so spoiled, they'd wake us up, sometimes even before Clyde did. Douglas called them Boos. "Boos!" he'd call out. "Boos!" I think they were his favorites because they were the least afraid of him. They might fly off when they first saw him, but after a bit they'd come back because they were stubborn about eating all the birdseed. Douglas loved to watch them. Sometimes he'd tap on the window, but he figured out pretty fast that they'd go away when he did that.

That night at supper, Mom started in about the temperature. "I know all of you think it's silly, but I worry about the birds when it gets this cold." She was dishing out spaghetti.

"I know you worry, honey," Dad said.

"I *do*," she said. She had me push the sleeves of her sweat shirt up out of the way because her hands were full. Sweat shirts and sweat pants were her favorite things to wear.

36

"Nobody's arguing," Dad said, and he turned to me. "Molly, would you argue with that statement?"

I shook my head.

"Douglas?"

Douglas shook his head.

"They're birds," Dad said to Mom. "Birds. Not lizards, not mammals, birds."

"Birds," Douglas said. He was dragging the mushrooms out of his spaghetti sauce. He likes to eat them separately.

"Paul—" Mom tried to stop him.

"Birds, although warm-blooded, have perfected a system of survival in these temperate zones—"

"Temperate?" Mom said, but he kept right on going.

"The secret is in their rapid heartbeat and the insulation of their down feathers."

"Paul"—Mom broke in, in her sweetest voice— "this is no time to start a lecture." She began to clear the table.

"Who's lecturing?" asked Dad.

"I know there are explanations for everything," she continued, "but I just hate to think of any living thing out there in that bitter wind." She shivered and rubbed her hands along her arms. "I had the sweetest pair of cardinals out there today. Remember, Molly?"

I nodded.

"This was the first time I'd seen the female, Paul. . . ." Her voice trailed off as she disappeared into the kitchen, and you could hear her fill the sink with dishes. "She was so skittish and *delicate*." She appeared in the doorway again to make her point.

"She'll be okay, Mom," I said, to try and cheer her up. "The seals live out there."

"What, honey?"

"Seals can live in the cold," I said. "They play in it. It's not too cold for them." I slid Douglas out from the table to clean his face and hands while she wiped up.

"When did you see seals?" Mom asked.

I was suddenly shy. "A little while ago, with Dad."

"Well, seals are different," she said.

"I know," I said in a low voice.

Dad bent over the wood stove to add another log to the fire and it made me want to run and jump on him for a piggyback, even though I was too old.

"Seals are unusual," Dad said, straightening up. I didn't even know he was listening. "They're warm-blooded, like we are, but uniquely adapted to freezing temperatures." He was wearing this big navy sweater

38

that I loved because it always smelled just like him. "Their closest land relative is the weasel."

"Thank you, Paul," Mom said. She grinned. "We needed that." She was always teasing him for talking like a book. "Your father," she'd say, "is a dangerous person to ask a question around." Her way would be for me to look things up in the dictionary or the encyclopedia. Dad's way was to launch into an answer ten times bigger than what you'd asked for.

Clyde sighed from under the table. No matter where he is, he always gives the same long drawn-out sigh.

"Want to go outside?" I asked him. I can get him up in an instant no matter how comfortable he is.

Clyde was up on all fours immediately, taking stiff, happy steps. "Watch out for his tail," Dad said. Clyde wags his tail like a propeller.

"Molly, you're not going outside in that cold, are you?" Mom asked.

"Clyde needs his walk," I said. No one else looked as if they wanted to budge. Dad was poking the fire and Douglas was sitting next to Mom on the couch so she'd read him the three books he'd picked out.

"Want to go for a walk?" I repeated. Clyde whined

low in his throat and stood over by the back door. He didn't take his eyes off me while I got dressed. He watched every move so I'd be honorable. Some dogs you could ignore and they'd go back and lie down after a while and still believe in you. But not Clyde. With Clyde, if you changed your mind, you had to say so— you had to say: "No walk now, Clyde," in a very firm voice—or he'd never take his eyes off you.

CHAPTER SEVEN

C H A P T E R SEVEN

It was bitterly cold outside, but crisp and clear. The snowbanks sparkled in the moonlight. I trudged along through the drifts, with Clyde bounding beside me. I wore a thick wool scarf wrapped around my ears, and my coat felt tight in the arms from all the sweaters Mom made me wear. I threw a stick for Clyde, and he dived for it and came up full of snow and knocked me down. I brushed him off and told him how he had to be good because we were going to look for seals.

"You have to be quiet, Clyde," I said. "You can't scare them." I tried to keep him nearby as we got closer to the bluff. The surf shone white in the moon-

41

light. I could see the long curve of the rocks stretching out into the dark of the ocean, but no seals. Just as Ruby had said.

"I want there to be seals, Clyde," I whispered. "I want there to be seals." I could hardly hear my voice above the pound of the surf. "Ruby had a seal once."

I told him the story over again, the way I remembered it, and sometimes my eyes blurred with tears, but that could have been the wind. I knew I should go back home, but I liked being there. As if it was a dare or something.

Can't you see me? I thought. Can't you feel me? I'm waiting for you. It gave me a lump in my throat. I'll be your friend.

There was nothing out there but rocks and sea.

Suddenly an awful cry broke out from the rocks below, like the wail of a baby. Clyde threw back his head and began to howl the way he does in the city when he hears a police siren.

"Clyde, stop it!" I held him tightly, partly for warmth and partly so he'd stay in one place. I looked out over the bluff, but I couldn't see anything. The cry came again, fainter this time.

"Come on, Clyde," I said, and began to run down the path to the beach. The wind was even stronger against my face as we moved closer to the shoreline. I could hardly see, but I aimed myself toward the rocks where I thought I'd heard the sound.

I saw the baby seal before Clyde did. I grabbed his collar to keep him close and he made that high-pitched whine. Something about her face made me think she was a girl seal. As I watched, she gave a sudden lift of her head in terror. I could see her tremble in the moonlight.

"It's okay, girl, it's okay," I murmured. She reared up a bit, as though she'd slide off away from us, but she held her ground. She couldn't have been more than a few months old.

I felt like walking over and picking her up in my hands, the way you pick up a puppy, but I didn't want to scare her, so I kept talking softly, the way I talk to Clyde outside the vet's office. "It's going to be all right," I said. She whimpered, and I wondered if she was hurt, but I wasn't close enough to her to see in the dark, and I didn't think she'd let me touch her, anyway.

"Hush, little girl," I said. She kept making those terrible cries. "I won't hurt you," I whispered. "I won't hurt you. Who's left you all alone like this? Where are the others?" It's worse, I thought, worse when a seal baby cries, because if she were a real little baby,

I'd know what to do. I'd pick her up and rock her. I'd held Douglas plenty when he was a baby.

I crouched to the sand so I'd be closer to her height. And then, for some reason, I began to sing. I sang "All Through the Night," because it's the one my mom sings to me, and the places where I couldn't remember the words, I made up new ones. She seemed to like it. She slid toward me a couple of inches. Then she lay still, almost six feet away.

That's when I heard Clyde bark. He gave his scared bark. It sounds very loud and angry, but I know he's scared. For some reason, when he's scared, I'm not, because usually he's barking at another dog, or a piece of kelp draped over a log.

"Cly-yde, come here!" I shouted. I turned to look for him, but I couldn't see anything in the darkness. When I turned back, the little seal was gone. She'd slid off into the water, without a sound.

"*Clyde!*" I called again, feeling miserable and frustrated. "You bad dog—" But still he didn't come. So I started to head back toward where I'd last heard him bark, feeling out each step so I wouldn't fall.

Just then I stumbled. Clyde had circled back to get me. He was barking at me, which he never does, and he smelled terrible. I followed him over to where the bluff rose up from the sands.

44

C. 2

At first, I didn't understand what I was looking at.

In the moonlight, the form of the seal was long and still, like a long piece of wood. I only really looked for a second before I looked away. I wish I hadn't looked at all. I think of it sometimes when it's dark. I hope Douglas never sees anything like it.

Then it slowly dawned on me. What if it's her mother? I thought, and then, just as fast, Please don't let it be her mother. My lips said the word *please* over and over but no sound came out.

The seal's head was crusted with sand, and its eyes were open. That's not how I knew it was dead, though. Its skin was just *gone,* as though someone had taken hold of it and pulled, the way you'd pull the bark off a tree.

I was crying. I grabbed Clyde by the fur at the back of his neck and made him walk with me as I scrambled for home. Clyde hated it. He likes to run ahead, but he let me hold on.

CHAPTER EIGHT

CHAPTER EIGHT

I burst in the door of the cottage and aimed straight for the fireplace.

"Molly, you're all wet," said Mom. "Brush the snow off first." So I ran back to the door and hung up my coat. "Boots, too," said Mom.

I took off my boots. I couldn't stop my teeth from chattering. I went and stood by the fire and stared into it.

"There's a dead seal on the beach," I said. "Clyde found it."

"How awful," Mom said. She was still reading to Douglas. "Are you sure, honey?"

"Yes. It's dead." I looked at her like I hated her for a second. "I think it's *skinned*."

"Skinned," Douglas said in perfect imitation.

"Oh, Douglas, you don't even know what it means," I said.

Dad looked up from his book. "I'm sorry. That wasn't a pretty thing for you to see." Then he frowned. "I'm surprised you found one where you did, though."

"Why?" I mumbled.

"Well, for some reason, I didn't think anyone was allowed to hunt seals here. I'm pretty sure there's a fine involved."

I didn't say anything, so he went on. "You have to understand, Molly. The fishermen here blame the seals."

"For what?"

"For ruining their nets." He took his glasses off and rubbed his eyes the way he does when he's tired. "Too often when the nets are hauled in, the netting is torn, and seals are blamed for it."

"So they hunt them down?" I looked at Clyde curled up by the fire. His legs twitched a little in his sleep.

"Fishermen lose a lot of money that way." The snow caked on my socks had started to melt and you could smell the wet wool.

"Seals are worth a great deal to these people," Dad said. "Dead, that is." I kept staring into the fire.

"They use the skin to make some type of leather. You'll see some of the old fishermen wearing pouches sewn from sealskin. It's considered lucky." He got up to add more wood to the stove, and the room got hotter.

"Well, it's not," I said. I could feel the heat of the fire on my face.

"Try not to think about it," Mom said. She closed the picture book in her lap, softly. Douglas had fallen asleep. "And hurry and take off those wet things— you look as if you've been sitting in the snow."

I got really quiet then, and obedient. I walked past everyone to the bedroom.

"Honey?" I heard her ask. But I didn't answer. I pretended that I hadn't heard. Everywhere I looked, I could see those horrible wounds. Even when I closed my eyes, I could see them. I sat on the bed and pulled off my socks. My toes were frozen. I tried to think myself ahead into a different season, one that would be warmer.

I went into the bathroom and took off everything else I'd been wearing. The tile was freezing. I took a long shower, but I didn't scrub. I just kept putting my head under the hot shower spray so that it plastered my hair down over my eyes. I started mouthing the words to the old lullaby again:

Sleep, my child, and peace attend thee
All through the night,
Guardian angels God shall send thee,
All through the night.

I started getting a lump in my throat again, so I closed my eyes tighter. I didn't remember the words to the middle part, so I made up new ones:

Guard her well, the tiny seal
Let her rest and let her heal;
Make her strong and [I ran out of rhymes] *make her heal,*
All through the night.

Later, when Mom came in to kiss us good night, she whispered to me how nice and clean I smelled. I gave her a little smile.

"It's a good thing Clyde was with you," she said. "You must have been frightened out there in the dark."

I nodded.

"Should I leave the hall light on?"

"Please."

She kissed my cheek.

"It was Clyde's fault," I said.

"What do you mean?"

"He barked," I said. "He barked and that's what scared—" I stopped suddenly.

"That's what scared you?" she asked.

I nodded. I couldn't say anything else. I don't know why.

CHAPTER NINE

CHAPTER NINE

The next day, Douglas was really getting on my nerves. Once he was down for his nap, I announced I was going to visit Ruby. Her door was unlocked when I got there, so I let myself in and went to sit on the couch. "Hi, Ruby," I called out. Instead of going into the kitchen to find her, I opened up the book I'd brought and started to read, even though I'd read it about eight times already.

Near the couch is a small lamp that Ruby sometimes lights on dark afternoons. The base of the lamp is a green china mermaid. The hands of the mermaid are raised as if they hold the light up. The whole mermaid is pale green. Even her face and hair are pale green.

I know that lamp has a story to it, but Ruby is a little funny about telling. She'll say, "Did I ever tell you the story of my mermaid lamp?" "No," I'll say. Then she'll start talking about something else. She can be like that sometimes, sort of mysterious.

Once I asked, "Well, is it a secret?"

"No," she said, "but it's *personal*."

"Is that you, Molly?" Ruby called out from the kitchen.

I didn't answer right away.

"Molly?" she called again.

"What?" I called back.

"Aren't you going to come in here?"

"I'm reading."

"What's that?"

"I'm reading a *book*," I called.

She came out into the sitting room. "Where's my kiss?" she asked, and I kissed her cheek. Her skin was dry and papery, and she smelled of powder. She looked at me suspiciously.

"Why such a long face?"

"I don't have a long face," I said. I stared at the base of the mermaid lamp. And besides, I thought, even if I do—it's personal. I tested the word out loud, in a whisper: "*personal*."

"What's that you said?" asked Ruby on her way back to the kitchen.

"Oh, nothing." I went back to reading my book, but it was hard to concentrate. Mom once told me that when Ruby was young, she'd fallen in love with a young man who was sent overseas to fight in a war. And though she waited and waited, he never came home. I hated war for that. I stopped reading and sat there watching the gleam of the lamp until I decided that maybe her young man had given it to her before he went away, and that was why she wouldn't talk about it. It gave me such a shiver of loneliness to look at the lamp after I made that up.

After about ten minutes, Ruby called out that she was making herself a bacon-mayonnaise sandwich.

"Would you like one?" she asked. She knew that I hardly ever got one at home because of the way the grease spatters all over the stove.

"Okay," I said. My stomach growled. I pulled up a kitchen chair while she cooked the bacon. The hickory smell filled the kitchen. It made me happy to smell the bacon and hear the grease pop. I couldn't help it then—I smiled at her.

54

"That's my goatgirl," she said. I knew the grease was stinging the backs of her hands. She wore a full apron with little tiny flowers all over the material and she wiped her hands a lot. *Goatgirl* is what she called me last summer. She said it was because my legs had gotten so long and she liked to see me scramble up the path like a spindly goat.

I sat in the kitchen chair and dangled my feet. I knew she'd push the toast down twice without my asking, and that she'd add extra mayonnaise for me.

"Douglas was impossible the other night," I said. "I had to give him a bath and every time I got near with the washcloth, he'd start to scream no-oo! I think he thought I'd get water in his eye."

"Did you ever get water in his eye?" she asked.

"The night before."

She laughed.

"By *accident*," I said. Ruby set out the sandwiches on plates and we both started to eat. You could see I hadn't exactly gotten sympathy about Douglas. As if the most horrible thing that could happen to a person was a little water in their eye. Well, a lot more horrible things could happen. A lot. My eyes filled with tears and I ate very slowly.

All the time I was sitting there eating my sandwich, I knew Ruby was waiting for me to say something else. But I didn't. I didn't care if she was trying to make me feel better.

Besides, it was so stupid. Now if I didn't finish my sandwich, she'd think I was sulking because of Douglas, and Douglas had nothing to do with it. I didn't want any more sandwich because the clear part of the bacon had gotten cold. I hate it when it gets like that. I thought about telling Ruby about my science project because she likes me to talk about school. But I didn't. I didn't say anything. I thought, I'll just leave and take Clyde out for a long walk. I'll just go off with Clyde somewhere. I'll walk and walk till I'm too tired to walk anymore. Then I'll just sit there with Clyde.

My nose stung at the tip. Oh boy, now you've done it, I thought. You're going to cry right here at the table.

I could hear Ruby clearing up, but I didn't raise my head. Tears dripped off my chin. I wasn't going to look up, though. I didn't make any noise, either. I didn't even let my breath out too fast. I never do. If you just looked at my back, you'd never know I was crying because I don't move at all. I can feel alone anywhere if I want to.

Ruby left for the sitting room. I could hear her

scraping cinders from the fireplace. It was worse without her in the kitchen. I started testing the soggy part of the crust with my finger. Even with my eyes closed, I could see the dead seal. Every time I'd think about it, my eyes would fill right back up, and I'd stare hard at what I was doing, mushing up my leftover toast. Stupid crybaby, I thought.

I wished I hadn't looked.

I got up and followed Ruby to the couch. She'd lit a fire, and the flames were crackling and sending sparks up the chimney.

"I wish I hadn't looked," I said. I sat in the corner of the couch, staring at my lap.

"Whatever are you talking about?" she asked. She looked at my face and put her knitting aside. "Come here," she said. "Suppose you come over here and tell me what's troubling you so—"

I moved over against her. "I *looked*," I said. "The seal was dead, and its skin was gone, and I looked. You said the seals were hunted on the far islands. You didn't say they were hunted *here*." I wiped my nose on the back of my hand.

Ruby pulled a Kleenex out of her apron pocket and handed it to me.

"Tell me what you saw," she said, and her voice was sad.

"It was just *dead*."

"But, Molly, they don't hunt seals here. There aren't enough. The men hunt where they can get skins—one hundred, two hundred skins a cull."

That word again.

"Well, I know what I saw, " I said. "And it didn't have its skin." There was a sharp hiss from the fire-place. "Clyde saw it, too," I said. "He's the one who found it."

"You poor dear," she said. "Come here. Come closer. You're right," she said, shaking her head. "It's an awful, awful thing." Her voice sounded odd and far away. "My father took me once, when I wasn't much bigger than you—"

"He *took* you—"

"Well, I hid in the dory." She took a deep breath to tell it. "I was a brave girl, you know, and I wanted to see things. Out by Sable Island, maybe fifty miles out, the harp seals lie out on the beaches. My brother and I had heard of so many on that ice, you couldn't see to stand." Her face was sad.

"You went on a hunt?" This was horrible.

"Well, you must understand, they didn't call it a hunt; they called it a *cull*. It's a soft word, for such a cruel trade." She shook her head, then looked at me. "I had no idea what it meant.

58

"The females were nursing, some of them." She spoke slowly with her eyes on the fire. "One or two bull seals were keeping watch. One, in particular, I remember by his bellow. And then the men went to work, my father and my uncles among them, and what was wild and still, but for the cries of the seabirds and the pound of the surf, became slaughter, and the ice all slippery with blood, and the keening of the mothers. Terrible sounds. Again and again, the long clubs hit—the little ones still alive mewling like kittens, and the dead ones, tossed like lumps of meat."

"I hate fishermen."

"Hush," she said. "In those days, there was a bounty on the skins. Five dollars a pelt. They did it for money and to feed their families." She sighed. "There's nothing ever that's all wrong, through and through. I should know."

Ruby began to hum slowly.

"Is it a song?" I asked.

She nodded and started to sing. Her voice was low and scratchy:

What never shivers
Nor sleeps in a bed?
 Seals of silver, seals of gold.
What is it dances

With sailors long dead?
   Seals of silver and gold.

"It's a very old song," she said. "There were many many verses, but only a few I remember." She hummed a little to get the tune and then sang again:

What's sleeker than satin
And finer than lace?
   Seals of silver, seals of gold.
What sinks without murmur
And leaves not a trace?
   Seals of silver and gold.

"There's a middle part, too," she said, and her voice cracked a little as she reached for the high notes:

What roams the salt waves
Yet will not draw near?
What haunts the shore caves
These dark silky years?

I began to hum along.

What waits by moonlight
Yet sings without fear?
   Seals of silver and gold.

There was a thud from the fireplace as the logs crumbled down.

"There was another seal, a little one," I whispered. "She was crying, just like you said. I got pretty close to her, but Clyde barked and frightened her away."

Ruby patted my arm. "Don't worry. We'll go look for her. She may not even be weaned yet, and she'll starve if she's truly separated from her mother." Ruby sighed and eased the edges of the afghan around us. "I still don't understand it. No one hunts here."

"I'd nurse her," I said. "We could use a baby's bottle. Oh, please, Ruby, let's go look." The clock on the mantel sounded very loud. I was surprised I hadn't noticed it before.

"But if we find her, you'll keep her a secret?" asked Ruby, strangely.

"Okay," I said. Then I thought about it. "Even from Mom and Dad?" I asked. "Because Dad is really good with animals—"

"Our secret," she said firmly.

C H A P T E R   TEN

"Show me where you found her," said Ruby. The sky was this funny pale gray. We'd taken the public steps down to the shoreline and approached from a different direction—Ruby couldn't manage the path. She had her cane for the steps, but out on the beach, she took my arm. From where we stood, the silhouettes of trees at the top of the bluff looked dark and twisted against the sky.

I frowned. It was already late afternoon. Everything looked different in that fading light. The sun was a low gleam. The sand was completely deserted, except for a few gulls, and the water was dull gray, like the sky.

"I don't see her," I said glumly. "She's gone." There were huge pieces of ice, the size of water coolers, knocking against each other in the waves. I went over to where I thought Clyde had found the dead seal, but there was nothing there, either. "It snowed," I muttered. The beach was almost flat, which meant someone had moved the body. I kicked away at the snow, as if I could hurt it. About three inches down from where I'd started was a deep maroon patch. I always thought that blood dried brown, but I guess this kept its color because of the ice.

"So much for your great idea," I said to Ruby. "She's *gone*." But Ruby ignored me.

"The cowards," she said, pointing toward a heap of netting near the foot of the bluff. I helped her closer. There were patches where the sand had drifted over the snow, and my feet kept slipping. "Hard to walk in these drifts, isn't it?" she whispered, gripping my arm tightly. There was quiet all around us, as though we shouldn't be where we were. At our feet lay a pile of old net, heaped against the start of the rise.

"Look at it—cut through and left to rot." She poked at the netting with her cane. "Not enough of a signature, though."

"Is it a fisherman's?" I asked. "Dad says fishermen *blame* the seals—"

"Well, it's a fool's blame," said Ruby, and her voice was bitter. "There's no net strong enough to bar a swimming seal—anyone knows it. It's the price of business in the herring shoals: one or two ruined nets a season." She bent and brushed at the snow with her gnarled fingers. "Smell that!" she said angrily, uncovering more of the net and a pile of dark brown bottles. It was a bad smell. She began picking them up, one by one.

"Here, Molly," she said. "Hold my sack open." And into the sack we'd brought to carry the little seal, she collected the bottles, draining the ones that weren't completely empty on the sand. "Those fools and their Guinness." She almost spat the word.

The sack was getting heavy.

"What's Guinness?" I asked. It smelled sour.

"Dark ale," said Ruby, "something like beer. It does the same job."

"Maybe we should go back now," I said. Dusk was falling and I could smell wood smoke on the cold air.

"It's the only explanation," said Ruby, "someone drunk enough to go hacking at a captive seal." Her voice was shaking. "I bet the little one was caught first," she said. "The older ones know better and are strong enough to break the hemp. But a mother seal would never leave her babe to drown in that viciousness."

"What do you mean?"

"Seals need to breathe, you know."

I nodded. I knew that.

"Well, a pup twisted in the net would be kept underwater. Can't breathe forever. The mother must have missed the young one, circled back, and broken through enough net to set her free—"

"Couldn't the mother swim free, too?"

"Not always. This one must have gotten tangled. So they hoisted her in, slippery, into the boat wale, and brought her ashore . . ."

Ruby paused. "And then they got good and drunk, while the seal lay heaving, all sandy and captive." There were tears on her face, but her voice was angry. "And then they came back for the skin, with the little one watching." I didn't know what to do—I had never seen an old person cry.

Ruby said we should mark the spot, to show respect. I put down the sack and went around gathering stones, filling my pockets with them and holding out the front of my coat like an apron to hold even more.

When I was done, I stumbled over to the place of the seal. There I made the stones into a marker, and Ruby helped. We had the pinker ones piled in the center, with rings around the pile in circles of different colors—white, gray, and gray-green. We made the final circle dark gray and black. My fingers ached. It was still bitterly cold, especially with no sun in the sky.

Just then I saw movement on the rocks, about twenty yards out. I felt frozen.

"It's the Great Bull Seal," said Ruby.

"How do you know?"

"From the marks on his shoulders—see"—she pointed—"see that darker patch, that's a scar there. One summer he was badly mauled by a shark. I wasn't sure he'd make it," she said softly.

"How do you know him?" I asked.

"I've known him since I was very young. . . ." She paused.

"The same one?" I asked—and when she nodded—"But how can that be?"

"Who knows," she said, but her mind was on something else.

"Let's go," I said nervously. "Dad says to be careful around the bull seals. They attack sometimes. You know, *bite*."

"He won't hurt you," she said softly. "He's in mourning."

"Ruby, *please*." I was shivering. "This place is getting creepy." The sack was heavy on my other shoulder, and we had a long stretch of walk back to the steps.

She took my arm, but she looked for a moment as if she wanted to say more. "He's been watching us," she said. "I think we made him happy with the stones." Her smile was hopeful and sad, all at the same time.

"That's dumb," I muttered. "How would you know?"

"Our secret," she said.

"*Ours?*"

"Not yours and mine. *His* and mine."

My teeth were chattering, and all of a sudden I couldn't wait for supper.

"Very funny," I said.

CHAPTER ELEVEN

The next morning I dressed early and went over to Ruby's with Clyde. It was still very cold, but the sun was bright and the sky was clear blue. Ruby had a fire going—I could see it through the window. I gave my special knock, but she took a long time coming to the door, so I pushed it open myself.

"Hi, Ruby, I'm here!" Clyde squirmed past me into the kitchen. He was so happy, sniffing every-where. "Ouch," I said. "Ouch, Clyde!" When he gets excited, his tail slaps against you and it hurts. I made him sit for Ruby and I gave her a big hug.

"Your fingers are like ice," she said, checking

them and rubbing them between her hands. I followed her into the kitchen.

"Have you had breakfast?" she asked. She had her hair in a bun. It was held in place with white bobby pins, and her scalp showed pink where her hair was thinning.

"No." I blew on my fingers to warm them. "No one else is up."

I sat at the kitchen table. The teapot was whistling and Ruby was spooning out oatmeal into a crockery bowl. Then, the spare-room door creaked open, and a *girl* walked in. "There's someone I'd like you to meet," Ruby said. I knew she meant the girl.

I stiffened. I didn't really feel like meeting someone at that exact minute. I might have felt different if I was meeting a friend of Ruby's—some neighbor or something—but this was a girl my own age. I felt horribly shy.

"Her name is Meara," Ruby said. "Meara is a Gaelic name—that's why it sounds a little strange to your ears."

"Meara," I said slowly, feeling out the sound. Meara. Like mirror-a. Meara, Meara, on the wall, who's the fairest . . .

"It's what was spoken long ago, in Ireland," Ruby continued.

"Do you know it?" I asked.

"I wouldn't be surprised if I knew a bit of it."
She winked.

"What does it mean?" I asked.

"Well, I'm not sure I know that."

She set the sugar and cream on the table. I looked
back at her for help, but she moved to the sink and
stood looking out the kitchen window to the sea. Ruby
says the windows are placed there so you can watch
the weather when you make supper. I guess it's true.
Our kitchen window faces the ocean, too.

"Hi," I said, "I'm Molly." Clyde began to thump
his tail against the floor, like he couldn't *wait* to be
introduced. "Molly Jane Bryson."

"Moll-y," the girl repeated slowly.

Clyde was making a big commotion. I said his
name so he'd stop. "This is Clyde," I said, and she
repeated the sound of it.

I sugared my oatmeal and poured cream slowly
over it, making little islands of oatmeal and rivers of
cream. Meara noticed and did the same. Her eyes
were blue, but not the way mine are blue. Hers were
light blue. Once I saw a kind of collie with one brown
eye and one blue eye. Meara's eyes were the same
blue as that dog's—light blue with a sort of hazel ring
around them.

Meara was the palest girl I had ever seen. She looked even paler because her hair was so dark—almost black—and against it, her skin gleamed like the underside of a shell. There was a blue vein that ran along her temple. The undersides of her wrists, too, had faint blue veins running under the skin. I know everybody has them, but, with Meara, it was as if she had a faint tinge of blue all over, like the color of skim milk at the top of a glass.

A sharp gust of wind made the windows rattle, and the noise startled her. When she turned to look, her hair caught the light, like a polished banister. It hung straight and glossy, except for the wisps around her face and forehead. There was a heavy purplish bruise running along her left cheek, and a small burst blood vessel etched in red.

"It's ugly," she said when she saw me staring. "Don't look." She covered the side of her face with her hands and her fingernails were shiny, like mother-of-pearl.

"Haven't you ever seen a bruise before?" Ruby said sharply. "It'll heal."

"I wasn't looking at that," I lied, and I could feel my face grow hot. "It's the starburst," I said, pointing to the red mark. "It's so pretty."

"You like it?" asked Meara. "Then I'll keep it

71

always." There was something about her speech that was a little odd, as if she'd been sick for a while or something and had forgotten the habit of talking.

I nodded. It wasn't fair of Ruby to act mad at me, especially in front of company.

"It's snowing again," Ruby said. She stood by the sink, rinsing out the oatmeal pan with her back to us—she was acting so strange, almost as though *I* was the stranger, and not this new girl. I looked out the window as I ate my oatmeal. I wondered if our stones from the day before would get all covered up and hidden.

"Will it snow a lot?" I asked, but Ruby just shrugged. I wanted Ruby to say something more, but she didn't. I wanted *someone* to talk. Otherwise, it was the two of us, just sitting there. I felt a little lost looking at Meara, the way snow can make you stare into it when it's falling.

"A terrible thing happened," I began. "Clyde and I found two seals." Meara was in the middle of clearing her place when I spoke. She moved stiffly, and it made me nervous. I wanted her to be looking at me.

"It was horrible—the baby one was crying, and the other one was dead. Somebody had killed it."

Meara did more than look. She dropped her oatmeal bowl the way you drop the lid of a pan when the

steam reaches your fingers. It broke when it hit the
floor.

Clyde rushed over to lick up the remains of the
cream and I grabbed at him to keep him away from
the bits of china and cereal. Meara held her hands
out in front of her as if they were burned. She took
two tottering steps, and then Ruby grabbed for her
and knelt beside her on the floor. Meara's eyes glittered
with tears even though she was staring straight ahead.
As if she'd just seen a car wreck or something. Ruby
called her name softly, but I don't think Meara heard
her. I don't even think she saw us then. Her eyes were
on some other sight that had swallowed her up and
swallowed the whole room up with her. That was a
really stupid idea of yours to tell, I thought. I watched
as Meara began to cry—a thin, high, almost soundless
wail. She curled her arms around Ruby's neck the way
sea foam curls over rock.

Clyde's tail beat time against the oak floor. Oh,
Clyde, I thought, let's not be here. I wanted to get
away from the sound Meara made.

But I didn't leave then. Instead, I sat down beside
the two of them on the kitchen floor. She's like me, I
thought. She loves those seals. She didn't want one to
be dead, and now that she knows about it, she's all
sad. My head started to throb and I felt pain along the

left side of my face, in the spot where her bruise was. She began to speak then—short, whispery syllables I couldn't understand. It was the only time I ever heard her make such sounds. She murmured them into Ruby's neck, over and over, as if she was saying someone's name.

CHAPTER TWELVE

CHAPTER TWELVE

The next day Douglas woke me up early. Usually when Douglas wakes up before I do, he just lies in bed making up little songs or talking to himself. But this morning he was right there tapping at the side of my bed. It was very cold, so I pretended to sleep.

Because it was winter, we'd brought double-thick wool blankets for each bed. The top blanket for Douglas is red plaid with thick black and yellow stripes. His hair is very blond still, and he looks so pretty when he's all curled up in that blanket. I can tell him he looks pretty and he won't make a face the way most boys would. He just laughs.

"Oh, go away, Douglas," I groaned. It's not very nice, but I've gotten into the habit with Clyde. Clyde is terrible for deciding it's morning before anyone else is up, and charging in on you nose first—like being nudged with a piece of wet peach.

Douglas kept tapping. Oh, Douglas, you are impossible, I thought—I'm so warm and cozy and if I move over to let you in, I'll have to stretch my feet down by the corner of the sheets where it feels like ice.

"Brrrrrrrrr," I told him, "brrrrrrrrrrrrr."

"Brrrrrrrrrrrrrrrrrrrrrrrr," Douglas repeated, and this made him laugh. "Brrrrrrrrr," he said, like a little motor. I threw back the covers and let him in.

Douglas snuggled against me and kept making the *brrrrr* noise and laughing.

"Oh, Douglas," I said. He shrieked with laughter then.

"Shhh, I'll tell you a story." That got him. I had to think fast now. Any story for Douglas had to have peanut butter in it, somewhere.

"Once upon a time, on a morning just like this, it began to snow. But somebody put a spell on the snow and everywhere it settled, it turned into *frosting*. Along the fence posts, it tasted like marshmallow, and on the tops of cars, it tasted like coconut. It tasted like cinnamon by the beach, and like caramel in the woods. Everybody begged to put on their coats and boots and run out for a snack. They packed graham crackers and apples and spoons. They had a feast.

"Guess who came, Douglas?"

"DOUGLAS," Douglas said.

"Yes," I said, "and birds came, too. Ducks came, and rabbits and foxes and dogs and horses and cats and beavers, too. It was a big party. Only one person was unhappy. Do you know who?"

"No."

"It was Douglas." Douglas laughed a little, but you could tell he was unsure of himself. "Douglas didn't want to eat marshmallow or caramel or cinnamon or coconut. He didn't want to just stick his tongue out and taste melted vanilla. He wanted peanut butter."

"PEANUT BUTTER," Douglas said.

"Everyone else was busy with the frosting, so he went off down the road. He searched everywhere. He searched mailboxes and doorsteps, wagons and flowerpots. He tasted park bench snow, picnic table snow, and water fountain snow, but he couldn't find any snow that tasted like peanut butter. Then he came back to the party and he asked his sister"—I started to giggle because I'd just thought of the ending—"he asked his kind big sister what to do.

"And she said, 'Why, Douglas, just go in the house and get a jar of peanut butter and mix it with the snow.' And that is what he did. He had peanut butter-marshmallow frosting, peanut butter-coconut frosting, peanut butter-caramel frosting, and peanut butter-cinnamon frosting." I kissed him. "The end, Douglas."

The smell of hot chocolate drifted in from the hallway. I could hear low voices coming from the kitchen and every so often, Ruby's name. Mom was making breakfast and Dad called for us to come sit down. When we were all at the table, Mom dished out everybody's scrambled eggs and toast. Dad gets the most and Douglas gets the least.

"I bet I know what you're talking about," I said. "You're talking about that girl staying at Ruby's."

"Oh, you've met her then?" Mom said brightly. "What's she like?"

"Okay, I guess."

Dad leaned forward on his elbows and gestured with his fork. "Well, I think that's great," he said. "It's nice for you to make a friend here your own age. Too bad we're not staying longer."

"I didn't say she was my *friend,*" I said. "I just met her."

"I wonder how long she'll be staying at Ruby's,"

Mom said, and she got up to pour herself more coffee.

"I'll have some, too," I said.

"No, you will not."

"Ruby lets me," I said, even though I knew Mom didn't think I was old enough to drink coffee.

"Well, your *mother* doesn't think it's such a hot idea."

"She may be staying indefinitely," Dad said. "Ruby says she's the daughter of some niece of hers. The family lives down near Gilbert's Landing, on the other side of the island. There's too much drinking going on at home," Dad continued, lowering his voice, "and some other problems as well. So Ruby offered to take the girl for a while."

"No other children?" Mom asked.

Dad shook his head.

"How sad." Mom sighed. "You hate to see it happen."

"Hate to see what happen?" I asked. "Are they getting a divorce?"

"Shhh," said Mom. "Not in front of Douglas."

"Ruby didn't say," Dad went on, still in that low voice. "But I wouldn't be surprised. Winter on the island can be hard on a marriage, with the fishing so poor, and not much to do but stare at walls and argue about bills." He helped himself to the last piece of toast and asked Mom to pass him the strawberry jam.

"Think of it, honey," Mom said, "no movie theaters, no shopping centers, no television—I bet this family doesn't even have a phone. After all, Ruby doesn't."

I nodded. "But *everybody* has television."

"Not on the island," Mom said. "People read at night, or tell stories—"

"Or argue—" Dad interrupted.

Mom ignored him. "It's just that there's not much to do here at night, and hardly any place open. None of the restaurants stay open year round—"

"With the exception of Dooley's Tavern," Dad said dryly.

"What?" I said.

"Let's drop the subject," Mom said before Dad could answer.

"I already *know*, Mom," I said. "I know about getting drunk."

"Nobody said anything about getting drunk," Mom said.

"But do you think they do?" I whispered.

"Whether they do or not, it's not meant to be discussed at our breakfast table," she said.

"What about Ruby?" I asked. "Ruby lives here the whole year round—"

81

"Ruby grew up on the island," Mom began.

"And for all we know, it may have been just as hard on her when she was young," Dad went on. "But she's lived here her whole life. She never married, never had to depend on the fishing season the way most of the islanders do."

"She told me she taught in the schoolhouse," I said, and Dad nodded.

"Whatever family she has," Dad continued, "lives on Ambrose—even if it's the other side of the island."

"Odd she's never mentioned them before, isn't it?" said Mom, clearing the plates.

Dad shrugged and got up to help her. "Not so odd," he said. "Anyway," he finished, "Ambrose is her home."

I carried the chocolate mugs to the sink and started to help get Douglas down from his chair.

"Have you done your thank-you cards yet?" Mom asked all of a sudden.

I frowned. Mom likes me to write to my aunts and uncles to thank them for my presents. The rule is: Finish the cards by the end of vacation. I like to decorate my cards and draw pictures on the envelopes, but it's not as much fun when someone reminds you.

"Not yet," I said.

"Well, I'd like you to try to finish them today, before you go visiting anyone," Mom said. "Is that clear?"

I nodded.

"Remember, we leave Sunday morning," said Mom. "So you really only have two more days."

"I can't believe it's Friday," I said, cleaning egg off Douglas's fingers, one by one. "We just got here."

"Doesn't school start Monday?" asked Dad. He loves trap questions.

"Just because school starts, doesn't mean *we* have to go back," I said. "Other people miss the first day sometimes."

"Your teacher doesn't miss the first day back, does she?" Dad teased. Being a teacher himself, he couldn't very well miss the first day of school.

"Very funny," I said.

I could hear Dad filling up the sink with water. Over the noise Mom called out that it might be a good idea if I started collecting my things so that there wouldn't be as much commotion on Sunday.

"Great," I muttered from the hallway, "we just *got* here."

I went back to my room and got my books and coloring pens all collected. On the window ledge, so I wouldn't forget, were my flower barrettes, my diary, my pink nail polish, and two new seashells, one a spiral shell that was hardly chipped at all. I had folded all my sweats and sweaters to stack on top of the bed, when Douglas walked over and started batting at my things.

Mom gave him a blank piece of paper and a blue coloring pen so he'd play quietly. The blue is *my* coloring pen, so you'd think she'd have asked me first, but I didn't say anything; I let him play with it. At least if Douglas tries to eat it, we'll be even. I'll get my pen back with chew marks but he'll have a blue tongue.

CHAPTER THIRTEEN

That afternoon when I went to Ruby's, Dad went with me. Douglas had caught some kind of cold and he was fussing a lot, so Mom stayed home with him. On the way over, Dad kept huffing and taking deep breaths and saying how great the outdoors was. He asked me if I knew the smell of balsam, and when I shook my head, he stopped by an evergreen, squished some of the needles in his fingers, and held them out for me to sniff.

At Ruby's he took his gloves off and pulled at one of the nearby branches. "Acorns." He smiled. "The blue jays love them." I knocked and Meara answered the door. You could tell she was surprised to see Dad. She wasn't dressed yet, and it was already afternoon. She had on one of Ruby's flannel bathrobes and it trailed after her when she walked. She wore long underwear, too—I guess it was Ruby's. It was way too big.

"I don't believe we've met," said Dad, smiling at her. "But Ruby's told me about you."

Meara didn't say anything. I liked her better for being shy with my dad.

"It's Meara," I said. "Her name's Meara."

"What a pretty name," he said, so she smiled. My dad can get anybody to like him. Ruby came in and made a big fuss over us, especially Dad, getting him out of his boots and coat and offering to bring out cookies for the occasion. "Helen couldn't make it?" she asked. And Dad said no, that Douglas was coming down with a cold and had to stay inside. "Well, I'll send some cookies home with you, then," said Ruby. She and Dad went on into the sitting room while I struggled out of my boots. I could hear them talking in low voices. Probably Dad was getting filled in on more details so he could tell Mom.

"Shouldn't we have cookies, too?" Meara asked. She looked worried there wouldn't be any left. I called out for Ruby to save cookies for me and Meara, and that made Meara laugh. "Cookies are the best," she said solemnly. She tried to help me get out of my coat by undoing my scarf and some of my coat buttons. It was hard to balance, though, with one boot on and one off, and I kept hopping on one foot, so as not to fall. It made Meara laugh even more, and she said this funny thing about how awkward I was. I kicked off my other boot and left my coat and scarf over the doorknob. I am not awkward, either, I thought, and followed her into the spare room so she could show me where she was staying.

We sat on her bed, eating milk and cookies, and I told her about making cookies, since she liked them so much. I couldn't believe she'd never made cookies before. "Your mom never made cookies?" I asked. She shook her head. I felt bad for her. "Well, Ruby makes them all the time," I said. "We can make some. It's not that hard. You mush the butter all up with the rest of the stuff and you put spoonfuls of it on the cookie sheet and bake them." Meara asked if she could try on my sweater. I had my rose-pink cardigan on over a turtleneck. It has glossy pink buttons to match the yarn. I could see Meara wasn't paying attention to much besides the cookies and what she could see right in front of her. She reminded me of Douglas that way. For example, she loved my sweater. She even loved my jeans and turtleneck. She loved *everything*. Every-

87

thing she could find, she would grin and call perfect. She even called *me* perfect. "Oh, perfect hands," she said, "perfect hair."

"It is not," I said, "it's all stupid and wavy—"

She ignored me. "Perfect, perfect sweater. Oh, shiny buttons, perfect buttons!"

She made me empty out my pockets for her. She was thrilled by pockets. I had a Doublemint gum wrapper, a piece of a shell, a red hair binder, and a folded tinfoil from yesterday. I remembered the day before when I'd told about the seal and it had made her cry. She didn't seem sad about anything today. She spread all my things out on the bed and said she liked the pink shell best, so I gave it to her. It was a broken piece, but it was smooth and nice to hold.

I asked where her suitcase was, but she said she didn't have one and that's why she didn't have anything to show me.

"I know lots of places here—" I said. Then I stopped. If she was from Ambrose, maybe the outdoors wasn't as big a deal to her as it was to me.

"You mean outside?" she asked. I nodded.

"Okay."

"We could visit the pond down by the General Store," I offered.

88

"Okay," she said again, and bounced off the bed into the sitting room.

She didn't act shy at all. "I have to get dressed for outside!" she announced to Ruby. Dad winked and stood up to go. Ruby walked him to the door and sent him off with a bag of cookies. Then she brought Meara shiny oilskin boots that swallowed up her knees. Meara pulled them on over the socks and long underwear. She was fun to watch. She belted one of Ruby's sweaters, wearing it like a dress, and wrapped a scarf around her neck. The way she held her head made you think of a cavalry charge. It made me want to run down a hill really fast with my legs pounding, or else sit close to her and have my chin lift like hers.

Then Ruby looked at her and said, "But you'll be cold," and Meara said, "Not me," and Ruby got quiet, the way you get when you call someone and the phone just rings because they're not home.

At the corner, we turned back to wave at Ruby. You could see the lace at the kitchen window move, but you couldn't see more than that, even if you squinted. I'm the worst squinter there is. It stings my eyes to be outside, especially in the winter. Meara didn't squint at all. Even with the sun sinking in front of us, she didn't blink.

I asked her why she didn't have any of her own stuff with her. "Did you leave in a hurry?"

"Yes."

"Are your parents going to send your clothes over, at least?" I thought a minute. "We have a car, you know, and we'll be here two more days. Maybe my mom and dad could go pick your stuff up."

"I don't think so," she said.

"Do you have a phone—you know, to call them?"

She shook her head. I didn't want to make her sad, so I changed the subject.

"Did you know Ruby from when you were little?" I asked.

She looked at me very carefully, then she nodded.

"I met her when I was *four*. She's like my grandmother," I said. "She's making me a sweater. I bet she'll make one for you."

Meara smiled. I asked her what grade she was in.

"You first," said Meara.

"Sixth."

"Me, too," she said brightly. "I like school."

"Really?"

She nodded. Maybe all six grades in one room is fun, I thought, especially when there's trouble at home and people talk about your parents in a whisper. Ruby says on Ambrose they still have a little red school-house, with only one teacher for all six grades. After sixth grade, children ferry to the mainland to go to classes.

"How did you get that bruise?" I asked as we walked.

Her blue eyes opened farther, remembering, I guess.

"It doesn't matter," I mumbled when she didn't answer. I felt bad for asking. I'm not sure what happened next, but she sort of tumbled me down in the snow and nosed her face in close to mine. I tried to pretend it wasn't awful, feeling the snow start to melt around my neck and seep down my back. I couldn't tell, by looking at her, if she had melted snow on her lashes, or tears.

"Look, Meara, I don't like you to knock me down." I dug beneath my scarf for the clumps of wet snow.

"I'm playing," she whispered.

"Well, maybe it's colder for me than it is for you." My heart was pounding.

"It is," she said, "it is colder for you, but you're safe."

Who knows what that means, I thought. I stopped trying to look at her and just looked up. Now that I'd settled back on the snow, it sunk down under me, like sand. It was *cold*. I showed Meara how to make a snow angel by lying flat and scooping out snow with her arms and legs: Scooping out arms makes wings in the snow, and scooping legs makes a long skirt. Meara got up first and shook herself. It sort of ruined her snow angel. She looked the way Clyde looks when he's trying to get water out of his fur.

"Watch," I said, and showed her how to get up slowly and jump out of the way so that the snow pattern stayed perfect. I packed some snow together in my hands and handed it to her. You could see the ridges of my fingers on the snowball.

She tossed the snowball as far as she could and grinned. She asked if I had lots of friends at school, and I said, not really. I explained about being a grade ahead. "I never see my old friends because they're in fifth grade. They have a different teacher. Besides, even if I see them, it's never the same. We can't talk about the same things."

My teeth were chattering. I looked back at Meara. All of a sudden I wished she could come home with me, to be my friend.

"What about new friends?" she asked.

I shrugged. I thought about how my homeroom teacher had made that fuss over me in the beginning of September, saying who I was and for everybody to be nice to me. Saying all that was about the worst thing she could have done.

The sky was getting that sad blue color it gets at dusk. You could see lights flickering at Ruby's and farther down the road. Meara and I went over to Clarence's store to pick out candy sticks. Neither of us had any money, but Clarence said we could owe him the twelve cents.

On the way back, we stopped at the pond to feed the ducks. Then we walked back to the edge of the bluff. You could hear the waves pounding.

"Oh, look, Molly—"

I followed her gaze out over the water.

"Look at the moon," she whispered. I stared up at it. The moon gleamed white above the water.

"Look," she murmured, "my same moon."

"Of course it's the same," I said. "Why would it look any different? This side of the island isn't any different—"

She ignored me. The wind lifted her hair and whipped it across her face. "I love this wind," she said in a hushed voice. "I love this moon. I love this sky—"

I looked up at the first stars.

"The *same*," she insisted, "it's all here." She

SEAL CHILD

brushed the strands of her hair back, away from where they'd stick at the corners of her mouth. "Don't you just love it?" she said. She started pointing out certain stars, but I'd never heard of them. She named each of the corner stars in the Little Dipper.

"That's the Little Dipper," I said. "Dad taught me how to find it from the North Star."

"The Little Dipper," she repeated. The wind blasted off the shore just then and it made her laugh. She opened her arms wide, like wings. The way her sweater caught the wind made me think of the webby part of a bat.

Meara called out something else then, but the wind swallowed it. I couldn't believe she wasn't cold—I could hardly feel my nose. She grabbed at my coat and pointed. Down below in the water, I could just barely make out loops and swirls of shine.

"What is it?" I whispered.

"Seals," she said.

I rolled my eyes.

"No, really, Molly, *look*—at night, the water lights up after them. Even if you can't see them in the dark, you can see the loops they make swimming."

"Are you sure?" I asked.

She nodded. Just then I saw a little head pop up, all silver in the moonlight. "Oh, Meara," I breathed.

"You were right—" Another head bobbed in the water, and I held my breath. Then they were gone, but you could see a trail gleaming where they'd been. It only lasted a few seconds.

We stayed there a long time. The ocean was dark, except for a glimpse now and then of shimmer. The moon shone so bright you couldn't look at it, any more than you can look right at the sun. My shoulders were all hunched up and my eyes were little slits against the wind. We're the exact opposite, I thought. The longer I stay out here, the closer I get to freezing. Meara looked as if she wanted to stay there forever, soaking up the bright moonlight. It was spooky.

I stamped my feet to keep warm and said how *cold* it was. Nobody would believe this back at school. Finally I shouted at her: "Meara!" and she turned. She looked startled for a second. "I don't think we'll see any more tonight," I said with my teeth chattering.

"Oh, Molly, you're cold."

"I am not," I said. But she knew I was, so she pulled me around in a ring until I was laughing and had warmed up some. Then she tagged me and I chased her all the way back to Ruby's.

CHAPTER FOURTEEN

C H A P T E R FOURTEEN

Ruby's windows were all steamed up so you couldn't see outside. Inside it smelled like pot roast and baked apples. The air was so warm, it seemed strange to breathe it in after all that cold.

When she heard us in the hallway, Ruby came out of the kitchen: "Just look at those rosy cheeks!"

"Ruby, we saw seals, right at the top of the bluff where you said to wait." I put my hands on my cheeks, they were stinging so badly.

"Did you now? That should make you happy," Ruby said. I looked over at Meara. Still pale.

"Yes," I said. "Now I know why you said to look for them by moonlight. It turns them silver—"

Ruby smiled. "Yes, moonlight turns them silver—"

Meara ignored us and ran ahead into the kitchen.

"—and daybreak turns them gold."

"Golden seals," I whispered. "How beautiful—"

"Mind you, I've never seen one turn gold myself"—Ruby chuckled—"but I've heard it can happen."

Meara had her candy sticks spread out on the kitchen table. She had all three unwrapped at once and was busy trying each flavor.

"What's this one?" she asked with her mouth full.

"Peppermint," I said, giving her a strange look. "Red stripes are peppermint."

"I knew that." She giggled. "My *favorite*."

I went to the stove and peeked under the lid of that big pot Ruby uses.

"Beef barley," said Ruby. "Taste it for me." I got one of the silver tablespoons she keeps standing in a glass and dipped it in.

"Mmmmmmm," I said.

"You sound just like your mother," said Ruby. She asked if I wanted to stay for supper, but I knew

I couldn't because Mom was making a big dinner. I shook my head.

"We're leaving Sunday morning," I said abruptly. Meara was standing in the kitchen doorway, looking dreamy.

"When will you be back?" she asked shyly.

"In the summer, as soon as school lets out," I said.

Ruby started rummaging for a plastic bag. "Never long enough," she said. "What was it this time, ten days?"

I nodded. Ruby filled the plastic bag with muffins and handed it to me. They were still warm. "Applesauce muffins—your mother likes them," she said.

I followed Ruby into the sitting room to get my coat. Meara stood off to one side, brushing her hair. Strands of it would follow the brush on its way back up.

"If I let it grow, how far do you think it will reach?" Meara asked.

"Let me see," I said. I put my coat down on the arm of the couch and brushed her hair back. I brushed it into a ponytail that I held in one hand. She was talking to Ruby about something, and the nod of her head made the ponytail dance. After a while, I let it fall to her shoulders and just brushed it straight. "I think you could grow it to the middle of your back if you wanted," I said.

"By the summer?" she asked. I wanted to say yes to please her, but I didn't think anyone's hair could grow that fast.

"If you're lucky," I told her. I made the ends of her hair curl over my fingers as I brushed it. It was soft and fine, like Douglas's.

"Meara says the seals leave trails when they swim," I said to Ruby.

"It's not so mysterious," Ruby said. "Did you see some?"

I nodded. "Sort of bluish-green and shimmery—"

"Yes, I know them. They're lovely, aren't they?"

I nodded again and kept brushing Meara's hair.

"Certain kinds of plankton are phosphorescent," said Ruby.

"You sound like Dad," I said.

"Once a teacher, always a teacher." She smiled. "Plankton are tiny one-celled plants. They float in the ocean, too small to be seen, and glow in the dark when disturbed. When the seals swim, they knock paths through that suspended phosphorous. By moonlight, their trails are luminous."

"Like silver," I said softly, and Meara smiled.

100

"Give my love to your parents," Ruby said, holding out my coat, "and be good to Douglas."

I am good to Douglas, I thought. Meara wanted to know who Douglas was.

"My little brother," I said. "You'll meet him."

"Good-bye, Ruby," I said, and hugged her. "Bye, Meara." It made me feel shy all of a sudden to be saying good-bye.

It was very cold when I left to walk home, even colder than before. I knew there wouldn't be any cars, but I walked on the side of the road anyway. My boots kept crunching the snow under me. I remembered the song Ruby had sung for me. I hummed it some and made my steps keep the rhythm of it. *Seals of silver, seals of gold, seals of silver and gold.* It was a little icy where I walked and my footsteps made a huge noise in the dark.

Suddenly I thought I heard another step following close on mine. I stopped to see if it was an echo or not. Complete silence. Doesn't prove anything, I thought. Just because the other sound stopped, too, doesn't mean there isn't someone out there, following. Imagining made it worse. Oh, please go away, I prayed, with my lips moving but no voice. I couldn't turn around, even to look. I took another step and the snow crunched under my foot. I didn't move or breathe.

Another step cracked close on mine, like an echo.

I ran so hard, my side hurt. I turned up our street and aimed with all my might for the yellow porch light, and ran smack into Clyde. He yelped, but he wasn't hurt. I fell on the gravel. I was lucky I had mittens on or I would have skinned my hands. Clyde was all over me, wriggling like a puppy and licking my face.

"Were you out looking for me?" I asked. I always talk to him out loud, but this night I talked extra loud. "What a good dog," I said, and stood back up. I looked behind me then, but the street was empty. Clyde was in heaven, wagging all over and trying to walk between my legs. I brushed myself off. "Come on, Clyde," I yelled. "Supper!"

I beat him to the door.

CHAPTER   FIFTEEN

C H A P T E R   FIFTEEN

It turned out that Ruby brought Meara over after supper, so Meara got to meet my mom, too. She would have met Douglas, but he was still sick, so he'd gone to bed early. Meara and I started to put on nail polish in the kitchen, but Mom said to take it somewhere else, because she didn't like the smell. She was making hot-fudge sauce while Ruby dished out the vanilla ice cream. Once we came back in with our new pink nails, the conversation stopped.

"What were you talking about?" I asked. Dad came in then for his bowl of ice cream and set down his paper. "Just talking to Ruby about something, honey," Mom answered.

"What about?"

Mom didn't answer right away. By then everybody was sitting in the living room. For a while all you could hear was the clink of spoons against the ice cream bowls. Meara loved hers. "You never had hot fudge before?" I whispered. She shook her head and opened her eyes really wide to show hot fudge was the best.

I heard Mom ask Ruby something about the dead seal, but I didn't hear what Ruby answered. Meara wouldn't look at me.

Dad asked if they were still allowed to hunt seals on Ambrose.

"No, it's not allowed," said Ruby.

"Could we please not talk about it?" I said.

No one really said much after that; we just ate our ice cream and Meara and Dad both had seconds on hot fudge. Ruby and Meara left after a while and, after they left, that creepy feeling that had followed me home came back. I'm not usually scared of the dark, but that night I was feeling so spooky I didn't even like to walk past the windows.

Clyde was on my bed when I walked into the bedroom. He jumped to the floor with a sort of guilty look and stretched himself. I don't mind it when he's on my bed—especially in the winter because he leaves such a warm spot—but when Mom sees him there, or on the couch, she yells at him. That's why he gets confused.

I grabbed at his collar and patted the bed so he'd get the right idea and jump back on. It didn't work, though. The thing about Clyde is that he doesn't understand about changing your mind. When he was on the bed, he wanted to be there, and now that he was on the floor, he wanted to stay on the floor. To get him back up on the bed, I had to trick him a little.

I made my hand into a fist and every so often I'd say, "Look what I have, Clyde, look!" and open my fist just a little to peek in, without exactly *telling* him I had a cookie. Then I climbed up on my bed and waited for him to follow, which he did. He jumped up after me and started licking at my hands. I scratched behind his ears and told him what a good dog he was. Then I caught a glimpse of our reflection in my window. That will prove it, I thought, if Clyde sniffs at the window and starts to whine about what's out there. I parted the lace curtains and looked out, but I couldn't see anything—it was too dark. My reflection shone back at me.

My nightgown showed up the best because it was

white. Clyde hardly showed up at all except for his eyes. They glinted a little in the window glass. My face looked ghostly and pale. It seemed that the longer I looked, the weaker I grew, as if whatever was out there could slip in under the window sash and find me, and I wouldn't be able to make a sound. I felt so strange.

Once, when Clyde was a puppy, I had him curled up with me for a nap and he turned in his sleep and scratched me across the cheekbone with his paw. It left a huge welt close to my eye and raised a thin line of blood. I felt as if I was doing that same mistake all over again—letting something in too close that would hurt me, by accident.

Mom brought Douglas back from the bathroom, in his yellow pajamas with the feet in them. He smelled sweet, like toothpaste. Clyde wasn't interested in the window; he was interested in Douglas.

"Is your stuff all set for Sunday, honey?" Mom asked.

"Almost," I said. I let her tuck me in, after Douglas. With her hand, she smoothed the bangs back from my forehead and bent over to kiss me good night. Her breath smelled warm and sweet, too. Then she switched off the light.

In the doorway, she turned back and asked if everything was okay.

106

"Of course," I said, so she smiled and closed the door behind her.

Douglas was fast asleep. Clyde was curled up like a hatbox at the foot of my bed. I was wide awake.

What if someone *had* been following me? I remembered the empty bottles of Guinness. What if someone started wondering who found the dead seal or who started all the talk about seal hunting on the island—I shivered. What if they asked Clarence? I was sure I'd said something to him on one of those visits to the store. What if he told? "Her name's Molly. Molly Jane Bryson. Lives down the road." Don't be stupid, I thought. It's not like witnessing a murder or anything, because other people don't think of killing a seal as murder. Except for maybe Ruby.

I thought of how sweet the seals had looked when Meara and I saw them from the bluff. But when I tried to think about Meara, it was strange because I couldn't remember exactly what she looked like. I could see her in my mind, but it was like remembering a certain look of her at a certain time. I had three pictures of her in my head: one from yesterday when she dropped her bowl, the way she looked when she opened the door for me and Dad at Ruby's, and the picture of her standing on the bluff. I couldn't remember her without one of those pictures.

107

I wondered if she'd be there in the summer when we visited again. Of course, she'll be here next summer, I thought, otherwise she would have said something. I turned over and sighed.

The picture of the silver seals came back into my head, the look of them, bobbing up in the moonlight. Then that picture would fade. I'd remember their trails disappearing after them, into darkness, and that creepy feeling would come back. The wind outside gave a loud moan and made the lower edge of my curtain tremble.

I wished Mom and Dad's bedroom wasn't so far down the hall.

Driving home tonight would have been better than waiting for Sunday. It's more exciting at night. We wave good-bye to the island on the last ferry out, and then Dad drives straight through. We have the back-seat all fixed up with pillows and blankets, and Douglas and I lie there with our heads at opposite ends, and Clyde in the far back. Mom and Dad start singing in the front seat, and Douglas and I sing along, too, the songs we know. I like to lie there and feel the hum of the motor. When it gets dark, the headlights of the other cars shine in and make jagged shadows; then they're gone.

Tonight, especially, I wanted to be riding in our

car, going *home*. The first instant I got in the back-seat—I'd push down the locks. I'd ask for the overhead light on if I was still scared. If they wouldn't turn the light on—Dad doesn't like it when he's driving—I'd say: "Oh, just for a second, I think I have a sliver." That way, when Mom checked, I'd be safe in the back, surrounded by love, and I wouldn't ask for anything else, no matter how dark it got. Except maybe an orange.

If right this minute we could all be in the car, I'd ask for an orange. Mom would peel me one in the front seat and hand me the orange in two halves. The whole inside of the car would smell like orange spray. I'd take the halves and separate them piece by piece into little boats and make a star of them on top of the blanket. I'd make the orange last a long time. I knew I'd be safe as long as anyone who might hurt me had to first watch me eat an orange. I didn't think anyone could want to hurt me after that.

I lay on my side, facing Douglas, with my back to the window. The last thing I thought of before I fell asleep was that it was stupid to sleep that way.

In my dream that night, there was a room, like our gymnasium at school, with painted circles, and free-throw zones, and a slippery floor. But it wasn't exactly our gym, because it was also like the inside

of a ship. From the way it rocked, I knew we were at
sea. The ceiling was low and there was a thundering
above me like when everybody changes classes and
the stairways are jammed and noisy. Then I forgot
about everyone upstairs because Meara came in a doorway at one end of the room. She held a tall white
candle and together we went around lighting candles
at all of the windows. The windows looked like the
window in my room, with the same kind of billowy
curtains. Once the candles were all lit, it looked beautiful, and we started a spin in the center of the floor
in one of those circles where you hold hands and lean
back and circle sideways faster and faster, till one of
you gets too dizzy. Suddenly Meara stamped her foot
and shouted and ran to one of the windows. "No," she
shouted, "no, no," over and over, and she pushed
against the window like someone was trying to topple
it from the other side. Then the window shattered and
the sea came pouring in with a crash. Once the window
broke, I didn't see Meara at all. The rest of the windows
broke and it was like dozens of fire hydrants all spout-
ing full blast, only the water poured in dark and salty
and there was no end to it.

That's when I woke up. I didn't know what time
it was, but it wasn't light yet. I was all sweaty from
the dream and my nightgown felt clammy. "Clyde," I

said, and my voice croaked out, rusty with sleep. He didn't move at first, so I kicked at him a little from under the covers. His side felt warm down there by my feet.

"Clyde," I whispered. I heard his tail thump then, and I could just barely see the shape of his head in the darkness. So I talked to him and he thumped some more and the next thing I knew, it was morning.

CHAPTER SIXTEEN

It was my last day on Ambrose. Meara and I walked the beach all the way from the public steps out to the breakwaters. I wanted to keep going, because for once, it wasn't that cold, but I could tell she didn't really want to walk the whole north beach. Later on, over at Ruby's, I finished up the last of my thank-you cards, and Meara decorated her own card and envelope to send to me in Boston. "Don't write it *yet*," I said, "and don't tell me what you're going to say." It took her a long time to understand that I wanted it to be a surprise, but once she understood, she agreed.

I told her my favorite colors: first pink, then red, then purple. She took a long time deciding when I asked hers. Finally she pulled the blue coloring pen out of the pack.

"Blue?" I said.

"I love the blue," she said.

I nodded. My favorite used to be blue.

"But it's not my *favorite*," she said. She drew fluffy clouds with the blue. Next, she chose yellow, for stars. "I can't pick my favorite," she said. "Because as soon as I take one out of the pack, it's never as beautiful alone as it was next to all the others."

"I know what you mean," I said. I showed her how to make a rainbow, because that way you get to look at all of the colors at once. When I was done, she smiled, and the part of me that was still icy from last night's dream warmed through, like snow melting.

When I woke up Sunday morning, it was just turning light. Dad was shaving in the bathroom and I could hear Mom feeding Douglas cereal. I grabbed my coat and ducked outside with Clyde for one last look at the shore. I fed him bits from my piece of toast on the way down. The beach was completely deserted and the ocean was quiet and gray.

113

I couldn't see anything where we'd left the stone markers, but I kicked away at the sand, like Meara stamping in my dream, and uncovered a stone or two. The sun began to glow on the horizon and slowly the whole ocean began to glow. Just then I saw movement on the rocks, about fifty feet out. I squinted to see better, and there he lay, the Great Bull Seal that I'd seen with Ruby. He seemed as long as a man, with darker patches on his shoulders. As I watched, the sun lit the waves beside those rocks, and, to my eyes, he almost shone gold. I grabbed Clyde, but the wind must have been wrong, because Clyde didn't notice anything—though he struggled to get free. I heard Mom calling, so I let Clyde go and he raced up the bluff like a glossy blur. I felt frozen again. I didn't know who would move first, me or the seal. Then, like something awful, I picked up one of the stones at my feet and hurled it as hard as I could at the dark gold head watching me. The stone clattered on the rocks and came to rest a few feet later. Long before it hit, the seal had slipped away into the water. No ripple. Just the ache of my arm, from having aimed so wildly, and the sound of the waves.

By the time I got back to the car, it was all loaded up and Douglas was already in the backseat looking at one of his books. Mom's voice had a sharp edge, asking me why of all times I was down on the beach when they were trying to get an early start. When she gets like that, the best thing to do is to give in.

"I'm sorry," I mumbled, but that just seemed to make her madder. After she finished yelling, it was like having a million paper cuts all stinging at once but too small to see.

I started to get in the car, but I couldn't make my knees obey. That's when I blurted out that I'd left something at Ruby's. I thought about saying that I *had* to say one more good-bye, but I knew Mom was already mad at me for making them late, and I worried that she'd say something to ruin it. It's like Clyde, in a way. There could be this beautiful june bug, dark and shiny-green on the sidewalk in the summer, and he'd just keep pawing at it. It depends on the luck of the june bug, then, if it gets away, because Clyde doesn't understand about hurting small things. He snaps at fireflies, too, though he always misses.

"Well, hurry!" Mom called after me as I ran down our street. I ran as if the running wasn't part of me, as if my arms and legs belonged to someone else. The wind rose in my ears like water and I thought of that great golden seal swimming somewhere I couldn't follow. Banks of snow sparkled in the sunlight. The whole morning was forgiven, I thought, except for me.

My eyes stung. Poor seal, I thought, poor seal to have stones thrown at you. But even if you hate me, you're safe in the water now, *safe*. Then I thought of the mother seal and the horrid net that trapped her. "Swim free," I whispered. "Stay far from shore. There are still knives on Ambrose."

Still, my throwing arm ached like an evil thing. I took a handful of wet snow and threw it hard at a tree trunk. It hit dead center and one whole shelf of icicles fell off the lowest branch. I've hit Douglas with that arm and Douglas loves me. He loves me the same every day, with no time out for being mad from yesterday or the day before. He loves me no matter how mean I am. Just wait, Douglas, I thought: I'll read to you in the car all the way home.

I saw Meara when I turned the corner, almost as if she was waiting. She sat on Ruby's stoop, tossing bread crumbs. Small gray birds, sparrows I guess, were feeding from her hands. She looked up and smiled, and I felt even more miserable.

"Meara," I said, "will you be here when I get back?"

"I'll always be here," she said.

I scuffed at a chunk of ice with my foot. "Dad says your parents live on the other side of the island."

She nodded slowly.

"Well, do you mean you'll be back with them or here at Ruby's?" I asked.

"I'm not sure," she said.

I stared at her. "But you'll write?" I asked.

"Of course," she said.

"Good," I said. "I will, too." I thought for a minute.

"If you've gone back to live at home by the summer, can I come visit you?"

"I don't think it's that easy," she said.

I stamped my feet on the ground to keep warm. "Just say *yes*, Meara."

"Yes," she said in one soft breath, and it was a magic word, like one you'd use to open a cave.

"I'm already late," I said. "I told Mom I forgot something."

She bit her lip, thinking, and then dug around in her pockets. She took out the little piece of shell I'd given her.

"Here, take it," she said. The inside was smooth and pink-colored, like coral. I hesitated. *"Yes,"* she

117

said again, and smiled, so that I saw it didn't matter who had the shell as long as we kept giving it back and forth, over and over. I hugged her and ran.

I slept a little bit on the car ride back. I didn't read to Douglas. I thought about it, but when he wasn't sleeping, he was playing with his truck along the bottom of the window.

CHAPTER SEVENTEEN

My sweater from Ruby arrived the first month we were back, followed by a letter that was all about Meara. I wrote back about ten times, but after that one letter, I didn't hear anything. It made me wonder if the mail was working. I couldn't wait for spring.

By April, I'd check our front yard each day for the first tips of crocuses. When I saw them, I whispered, "Oh Meara, how beautiful." Because I knew she'd just love them. The white and the purple, and even yellow, all together against the green leaves. Sometimes I might not say anything—like when I saw bright red petals of tulips—but there would be a quick

119

little breath in my heart, and I'd want to tell *her*, and I would, too, but in a quiet way, like thinking.

On the days when it rained and I had a terrible time walking to school because of all the earthworms on the sidewalk, I'd think of Meara, sipping tea with Ruby, and I'd long to be there, just the three of us. I wasn't so bothered anymore that all the other girls already had their best friends picked. I didn't mind it when Donna Lindstrom chose Beth Ryle for pitcher at softball, or that Jeannie Allen always sat next to Sarah at assembly, or that Robin and Lorrie were friends from kindergarten and everyone knew it.

If I was bored in school, I'd think about braiding Meara's hair, which she said I could do in the summer. I'd make two long braids and weave them together with shells and blossoms. Ruby has a picture of herself as a young girl with her hair done up in garlands. Sometimes she'll take the picture off the mantel and look at it as if it were a fairy tale to her.

Once at lunchtime Donna Lindstrom caught me daydreaming. I had bought one of those giant chocolate chip cookies and broken it in two, placing each half on a separate napkin.

"How come you do that to your cookie?" she asked.

I made up some answer, but my face turned hot.

The truth was, I always made two halves, one for me and one for Meara, and while I daydreamed, I'd nibble some from my half, and then some from hers, and make us have a conversation in my head.

After Donna left, I pulled Ruby's letter from its envelope that Meara'd decorated with bright clouds and stars. I read it over for about the hundredth time:

Dear Molly Jane,
    I'm sitting here by the firelight, with Meara at my feet, and she says to be sure to say hello to you, and tell you that she misses you, and that I am making her a sweater to match yours, so that next winter you'll be twins. Meara wants to know how you liked the package we sent or if the cookies were all broken, and to tell you that her hair is much longer, and that she has a million more things to say, and would write herself but her handwriting is *awful*.
    Mind you, that's what she says. As for me, all is well. The blue jays your mother spoiled still come round for their birdseed. Along with one sweet pair of cardinals.
             My love to all,
               Ruby

Later that day, we saw a film in science class, but the projector broke down in the middle of a bunch of earthworms. Someone snickered. Probably Jeremy.

121

I started a letter to Meara in my science notebook, though I couldn't see that well because the shades were drawn.

Dear Meara,
    I miss you. I hope you miss me. I wish you could come to my school.
    This morning I was late! Which is really horrible because if you are, everyone stares. I had to run my fastest the whole last block and got there just as the bell rang!!!
    It would have been fine if no one saw. But the stupid door monitors were there. They're supposed to stand by the front door and make sure everyone's in on time. Don't you just hate that? From when they first saw me at the end of the block, they started making fun. They kept yelling LOOK AT HER RUN, like I was really dumb for trying so hard.
    They couldn't leave it alone, either. They had to march me all the way down the hall into homeroom and I hated them the whole way. I was so mad I'd let them see I cared about anything.

I bit at the end of my pencil and my cheeks burned.

I started a daydream then, only in my dream I looked more like Meara. I did the whole thing over, but this time I walked right by those stupid boys and ignored the things they yelled. I reached the doorway after the bell rang, but they had to stand there and wait for me and it made them late, too. As I walked into the building, I heard them whisper to each other, wondering who I was to walk that way and not mind them one bit.

Just then, the teacher started up the aisle, so I covered what I'd written.

I knew we wouldn't be back to the seashore until summer, but in my heart I felt as if spring had come so soon, and spring was almost summer, and I could stare down eight million boys till then and run faster than any of them.

CHAPTER EIGHTEEN

The night before we drove back to the shore for the summer, I was too excited to sleep. Douglas wouldn't sit still for the whole trip. Every so often I'd ask Mom how much longer and I'd jiggle my knees so we'd get there faster. It was just the four of us in the car—me, Mom, Douglas, and Clyde. Dad had to stay in Boston to teach summer school. But he'd come up weekends to visit and he'd be there the whole month of August.

The ferry took forever, but the ocean was blue and shining. There are three turns in a row just before our road. I had both windows rolled down in the back so I could smell the salt air. When we finally stopped,

I jumped out of the car barefoot and had to hop because the road was so hot.

"Make sure Douglas gets his shoes and socks on," said Mom, so I sat back down and started fitting his sneakers on and jerking his shoelaces into place.

I could see a bunch of flowers on our doorstep. It looked as if someone had tried to prop them on the doorknob and they'd fallen down by themselves. I felt the way popcorn kernels must feel when they're sizzling. Mom looked at me as if she wasn't sure where I'd start popping first, at my knees or at my elbows. Then she laughed. "Oh, go along, we'll unpack without you."

Clyde was running everywhere with his nose to the ground, tracing squirrel trails. He caught up with me on my way over to Ruby's and loped beside me, carrying a stick in his mouth.

Meara sat in the field next to Ruby's cottage, weaving flowers into a wreath. When she heard me, she scrambled to her feet and the flowers tumbled out of her lap.

"Molly?" she whispered. She put her head to one side the way a bird does when it wants to know what you are.

"Meara!" I called, waving, and she smiled and waved back. By that time, I was beside her, and Clyde dropped the stick at her feet. Her hair was much longer, and it seemed impossible that it had grown so long.

"I've been asking Ruby if it was summer yet," she said, laughing. "Every day!" She wore a thin flowered shift with deep pockets, and they bulged on her like the sides of a carpenter's apron.

Clyde started to bark, the way he does when he wants to be included, and that made Ruby come out of the cottage.

"Molly!" Ruby called, "let me look at you." Ruby came over to me for her look and the sun beat down warm and golden. Clyde kept barking, and Meara just laughed and clapped her hands.

"You're taller," Ruby said when she'd finished looking. I stood back to back with Meara, and sure enough, I was a little taller. Meara was perspiring under the straw sun hat she wore. I could tell she didn't like the warm weather as much as I did.

"I missed you," she said.

"I missed you, too," I said shyly, and above the pattern of her shift I could see her flush and the rose color move up into her face. It surprised me in a way, because Meara was always so pale.

We walked farther behind the cottage into the field to pick flowers, and Ruby spread out a blanket over the long grass for us before she went back inside. We sat together on the blanket and Meara began twisting flowers together for the wreath. She said Ruby had shown her how to make them, and that she would teach me that afternoon. I lay back flat and let the sunlight seep into me.

"Meara?" I asked dreamily with my eyes closed. I could hear all sorts of birds chirping and calling and the sound of wings from close by. "Meara, are you happy?" I don't know why I asked, because I don't usually think of things like that, but I wanted her to say she was, so that her saying so could be part of the bright sun on my face.

"Yes," she said. I peeked at her through my eyelashes. "Look!" she said in a hush, because just then a cloud of white butterflies rose from the field. I squinted to see them and it *was* very beautiful. "I love the butterflies," she said. She went on to tell me how the Tuckers' ewe had had a baby in the spring, and that she'd gone to see it with Ruby the day after it was born.

"The mother wasn't very pleased to see us"—she grinned—"but the little one had no fear. Such a sweet little pup!"

"Lamb," I said automatically, and cuddled deeper against the warm ground.

"What?"

"You said 'pup,' " I told her, "but a baby sheep is a lamb."

"I *know* that," she said. "That's what I meant. *Lamb*." Then she got quiet. I looked at her and she looked sad. I didn't know why.

"I miss the pups," she said, and she buried her head in her arms and wouldn't talk anymore. I couldn't understand what she meant. "I miss the little pups," was all she'd say, and I couldn't get her to say anything else, even when I begged her to tell me what the matter was. Clyde came over. He had that happy look he gets from chasing bees and there were bits of burr tangled in his fur. When Meara saw him, she threw her arms around his neck and began to cry softly.

The wind picked up a bit. I couldn't see Clyde's face, the way Meara clung to him, but he stood his ground like an old cart horse. I don't know how he could act so patient. Even though he's so big, he's still really half-puppy. His tail began to creak back and forth slowly—not really wagging but letting me know he hadn't forgotten me.

I saw Douglas rustling through the clover. He thinks it's a great game to try and find me. Mom must have brought him with her, which meant she was over visiting Ruby. I tapped Meara on the arm and whis-

pered, "Someone's coming." She raised her head up from Clyde's neck. Her cheeks were streaked with tears and her great blue eyes wavered when she tried to look at me. So she gave up and stared at the flowers in her lap: clover, Queen Anne's lace, and white and purple daisies. The bees hummed from everywhere, but they didn't bother us.

Douglas wasn't having the easiest time getting through the tall grass. I heard him call from about ten feet away, though you couldn't see him too well from where we sat.

"Over here, Douglas," I said, and there were all these thrashing sounds as he struggled through the meadow. He's pretty good, Douglas. I don't know if I'd walk through a meadow that was taller than I was.

Douglas found us and stumbled forward onto the blanket. He threw himself at me in triumph and lost his balance and sort of spilled over by Meara. He was wearing a pair of red trunks and sneakers, and he stank of insect repellent. Douglas is still pretty round and soft. He has dimples at his knees, just like a baby's.

Meara brightened up all over when she saw Douglas. I've never seen anybody switch as fast as she could, from storm to sun.

"Why, who's this?" she said to him, and she took

130

his hands before they were even introduced and kissed them and kept laughing and saying, "How sweet you are!" over and over. I don't even know the word for how I felt. I mean, it was just Douglas. I told her so, too.

"Meara," I said, patiently, "this is Douglas. This is my little brother." But she wasn't paying attention. Neither of them were. Douglas is shy with strangers, so I couldn't figure out what was going on. But he was laughing at the sounds she was making and looking at her the way he looked at the candles on his birthday cake when he loved them too much to blow them out.

CHAPTER NINETEEN

I left Douglas there with Meara and got up to go into Ruby's. I called out that I was thirsty, but nobody paid any attention. I let myself in, and the screen door swung back on me so fast, it clipped the back of my heel.

"Don't slam the door," Mom called from the kitchen.

"I didn't," I said, and I checked my heel to see if I should tell anyone I'd hurt myself.

Ruby was sitting with Mom at the kitchen table. Ruby had the French bowls out that she uses when she drinks coffee.

132

Ruby makes this kind of coffee that she says is the French way. She heats milk and pours it in her bowl, half-full. Then she pours coffee into the hot milk. When she pours in the coffee, the white of the milk and the brown of the coffee swirl like speeded-up pictures of clouds. She makes it for me sometimes, and I add lots of sugar and stir it with a spoon.

When I saw Ruby, I said that I'd like some coffee, too, please. Mom almost said no then because she doesn't like me to drink coffee. She didn't, though. Ruby pulled out a chair for me at the table, as if it was completely natural for me to join them. "Just this once," said Ruby, winking at me. She got up—a little slowly because she gets out of chairs slowly—and began to fix more milk. I heard the sound the burner makes when Ruby lights it with a match, then the hiss of the milk as it hit the bottom of the pan.

"Meara is out playing with Douglas," I said in a perky voice so no one would think I was jealous.

"Did you leave the flowers on our doorstep?" Mom asked Ruby. Her fingers had begun to make a little pile of the crumbs scattered near her plate, as if her mind was on two things at once. "Or was it that grand-niece of yours? Molly talks about her so much."

Meara, I thought, her name's Meara, and I don't talk about her.

133

"That must have been Meara," Ruby said. "I haven't been down that way."

"What's it like having her here?" Mom asked.

"No trouble," said Ruby, pouring the milk into our coffee bowls. I added three spoonfuls of sugar. Ruby told my mom that it was truly a pleasure to have someone around—that Meara was such good company, and that she'd been a big help, especially in the winter months.

"Any word on how much longer she'll stay here?"

Ruby shook her head and finished pouring the coffee. Mom said that she'd heard Ambrose had a late spring—with snow clear through April.

I couldn't believe that Ruby was through talking about Meara. I kept stirring my coffee, as though the sugar wouldn't dissolve, and every so often, I'd taste a spoon of it. The way I saw it, if Ruby had just answered a little bit, then Mom would have asked another question, and it could have gone back and forth for a while. But the way Ruby answered, Mom wasn't curious anymore. I was, but I always wanted to learn new things about Meara, and save them, like I did with special shells.

Then Mom borrowed a sheet of paper and started making a shopping list for things to buy at Clarence's. Shopping on Ambrose was usually one of my favorite things because I got to help pick food out, like potato chips, or Hershey kisses, but right then, I didn't feel like shopping—all I could think about was how I'd really rather be outside, making flower wreaths.

By the time I looked down again, a big skin had formed on top of the milk. I lifted it off with my spoon and looked for a place to put it. Mom saw me and slid her saucer over. She smiled because she knows how much I hate that part. Mom asked if I'd go shopping with her, and Ruby offered to watch Douglas. I didn't exactly answer yes; I just got up to leave when Mom did. The windows were open and you could hear Meara laughing. Douglas, too.

"Sounds like fun," Mom said, with a wink at Ruby. It might be a little fun to play with Douglas, I thought. But not more fun than playing with me.

Just before I got to the door, I felt Ruby pull at the back of my T-shirt.

"What?" I said. She pressed something cool into my hand.

It was a wild strawberry.

CHAPTER

By the time we were done shopping and putting everything away, it was late in the afternoon. I looked everywhere for Meara, but I couldn't find her, so I went back over to Ruby's and let myself in. Ruby sat on the couch, reading. She peered at me over the tops of her glasses and motioned for me to come sit down.

Nobody said anything for a while.

"Nice to be back?" Ruby asked, so that I'd start to talk, but I didn't. I stared down at the strands in her rug, trying to imagine Ruby picking out the colors.

She took off her glasses then and placed them on

136

the end table next to her book. "There's something the matter, isn't there?"

"No," I said. But she didn't like that answer.

"You can do three things. . . ." She paused and her voice sounded tired. "You can chew, you can swallow, or you can spit it out, whatever it is. But you cannot just sit there."

"Where's Meara?" I said finally, but I didn't look at Ruby. I stared at the very center of the rug where she'd picked reds and maroons to braid together.

"Outside somewhere with Douglas," Ruby answered. "Why?"

I shrugged. "No reason in particular," I said, untying my sneakers, "but we were supposed to meet up here. She said she'd teach me to make flower wreaths." I tucked my feet up and sat cross-legged on the couch.

Ruby sighed. "Well, I can teach you, if that's what's bothering you."

"It's not the same," I muttered.

"What's that?"

"*Not the same*," I said, with my eyes on the rug.

"Listen to me," Ruby said.

"I am listening," I told her in a low voice.

"Molly," she said dangerously, "stop this right now."

"I *am* listening," I repeated.

Just then the front door burst open and Meara ran in all out of breath. There were bits of grass in her hair and two bright pink spots at her cheeks.

"We are so thirsty!" she announced to Ruby, marching directly into the kitchen. "Is there lemonade?" On her way back out, she saw me and stopped, balancing two glasses of ice in the one hand and a plastic pitcher of lemonade in the other. I knew she'd forgotten the wreaths.

"Molly!" she said happily. "Come play! Douglas is teaching me somersaults."

"I'm too tired," I said, frowning.

"Too tired for somersaults?" Meara said, astonished. Then she smiled and ran back out the front door, leaving it open wide.

"Meara!" called Ruby. "Mind the mosquitoes!" We heard her run back. There were more huffing sounds as Meara stuck her head in the doorway, breathless. She took one look at Ruby's face, grinned happily, and swung the door shut behind her.

Nobody said anything for a while. Then Ruby cleared her throat and spoke: "Are you jealous, Molly Jane?"

I nodded slowly.

She sighed. "You are making yourself suffer."

I felt my jaw set in a stubborn way, even though I wanted to please her.

"You are making yourself suffer," she repeated, "and there is no reason for it." She sighed. "No need."

"Well, I have a reason," I said.

That made her laugh.

"You really are very sweet," she said. Then she cleared her throat and shifted her position slightly.

"Meara is not meant to hurt you," she began again. "Meara is a gift." I started to speak but she motioned for me to keep silent. "Meara is a gift for many reasons," she continued, "and some of them I can't tell you and some of them I don't know. Perhaps, most of all, she is a gift because we love her and because it is so easy to love her."

"It is not," I said.

"Hush," said Ruby, and drew me closer. "Meara has been raised . . ." Ruby paused, searching for a word. ". . . Differently, you know, and she doesn't blame herself for her . . ." She paused again, searching. ". . . Ignorance.

"Sometimes she'll steal outside when I've fallen asleep—as though the moon itself drew her. I've had to scold her for it because she forgets to close the door, even in the dead of winter. Many nights I've woken to the cold, the red coals of the hearth little help against the open front door—" Ruby smiled, remembering the picture of it.

"At first I felt bad about scolding her, but Meara seems happy at these lessons, *any* lessons. She'll run back full of remorse when I call. 'Did I forget *again?*' she'll ask, and rush to me for forgiveness, laughing and pressing her face against the folds of my wrap.

"When she says over and over 'I forgot'—to her there is laughter in the lesson, laughter in learning anything. You must remember this, Molly—"

"Remember what?"

"To be happy—no matter what you're learning. And if the next lesson for you is that Meara is making a new friend and that new friend is your brother—"

"Little brother." I frowned.

"Well, be *happy*. Don't try to make her feel ashamed. It would only confuse her. Do you think love, real love, is ever a mistake?"

I didn't say anything.

"Molly Jane!" she exclaimed, exasperated. "You must answer people when they ask you something."

"Why?"

"Because it shows respect."

I frowned again. Ruby gave me a sharp look, then smiled to herself and shook her head. I heard her fingers rustle through the glass jar on the end table.

She leaned over, handing me a lemon drop and popping one into her own mouth. We sucked on our lemon drops long enough to melt through the sugar crust.

Ruby began to talk again, quietly. "Meara is learning about Douglas now, and she is happy. It is not for you to teach her this long sour face of yours so that she has to wonder what kind of mistake she's made—what new door she's left open to the cold."

"But she's been with Douglas *all afternoon*," I insisted.

"Oh, Molly," Ruby said, and it felt awful to disappoint her.

"She *has*," I said glumly. I felt like I'd just reached under my desk at school and felt all the old gum with my fingertips.

"Meara has some sort of light in her," Ruby said. "And she offers it to us, without knowing so. Sometimes I think she stores it up from the moon on those walks of hers. It will not empty from her easily." Ruby was turning her namesake ring around and around with the fingers of her right hand. It had a single red stone in the middle with two little pearls on either side. "Love like that isn't meant for any *one* person."

"Nobody's trying to empty her out," I said.

"Every choice she makes empties her," Ruby said in that same quiet voice. She pulled at her ring

141

then, as though she meant to pull it off but her knuckles were too thick to ease it over. Just as I thought how that must hurt her, she spoke again: "Would you test her, make her choose between two things she loves any sooner than she has to?"

"What do you mean?" I asked.

"She loves you both, you know, both you and Douglas. Why ask her to choose between you? Remember, she may not stay with us forever."

"I *know* that," I said. "But she just lives across the island."

"Let's hope so," Ruby said, taking my hand in hers. "But there's nothing that's for certain." She smiled sadly and sighed. "It's good you love her so, but remember, there's no love without danger, not true love."

"What do you mean?" I said. But Ruby was silent, and from the way she looked, I could tell she was done talking.

142

CHAPTER TWENTY-ONE

CHAPTER TWENTY-ONE

Later that night when Douglas and I were already in our beds, he asked me a question. His voice sounded a little thick and I wondered if he was getting a cold.

"Why can't she go in the water?" he asked. I knew he meant Meara.

"What do you mean?" I asked. With Douglas, you can never tell if he'll answer what you ask. Sometimes he answers a different question.

"We found sand crabs," he said, "lots." That started him laughing.

I propped myself up on my side and asked again.

"Douglas, why do you say that Meara can't go in the water?"

"She *can't*," he insisted.

"I know, Douglas," I said, "but why do you say that?"

"She can't swim with me," he repeated. "She *said*."

"Well, maybe she can't swim," I told him. Then I saw how that didn't make any sense because Douglas doesn't swim—he just splashes in the bay.

"You mean she won't even go near the water?" I asked.

"She can't," he said, and then, as though he hadn't already asked it, "Why?"

"I don't know, Douglas," I said. "I'll ask her, though." His breathing grew more regular then, and within seconds he was asleep.

I waited an extra few minutes and then I slipped out of bed and grabbed my sneakers. Clyde padded softly into the bedroom as I laced them up, but he didn't seem surprised; he just settled to the floor with a sigh and closed his eyes.

I tiptoed across the hall floor and let myself out

the front door. The night was clear and warm, definitely summer. I didn't even need a sweat shirt. I crossed the field behind our house and took the dirt path down to the pond.

Meara was sitting on a large rock ledge by the edge of the pond. The water hardly rippled.

"How did you know I was here?" she asked.

"I didn't," I said. "I just felt like a walk."

"Come sit by me," she said, and squirmed sideways to make room for me. I took my sneakers off and dipped my feet in the water.

"Cold!" I squealed. I sat that way for a while, dangling my legs over the side of the ledge. The sound of the water lapping was the only sound.

"Douglas says you can't go in the water," I said.

"He told you that?" she said, and she gave a small chuckle. "This water is fine." She smiled, and without another word she stood and dove into the pond. Her nightgown streamed behind her. She broke the surface about fifteen feet from me, gasping with delight. "It's *perfect*," she said. "C'mon, Molly!" I followed in after her, though I knew it would be freezing. The pond is spring-fed and there are pockets that are icy even in the middle of August.

"How come you're not cold?" I said as I paddled toward her, my teeth chattering.

"I don't know," she said. "Race you!" And she did a sort of surface dive and swam toward shore underwater. I followed behind. She was much faster. I didn't really like putting my head underwater at night all that much. The odd thing was that I could see Meara's hair gleaming behind her in the water, like phosphorous.

We pulled ourselves back up on the rock. I sat there with my arms wrapped around my knees, shivering, while she wrung out her hair.

"So, how come you told Douglas you couldn't go in the water?" I asked.

"Because we were at the beach," she said happily.

A chill went through me.

"What do you mean?" I asked.

"This is fresh water," she explained. "I can swim in fresh water. Just not in the ocean."

"What do you mean?" I asked again, and my voice sounded a little shrill, even to me. "Are you scared of the ocean?"

"A little," she said, leaning back against the rock face and looking up at the stars. I thought maybe she'd

almost drowned once or something. I remembered getting plowed under by a huge wave and swallowing lots of salt water. It could be really horrible, the ocean.

"What do you mean?" I asked for the third time, but she didn't answer.

With another person, you'd think it was rude if they didn't answer you, but with Meara, it wasn't that she was being mean about it, she just stopped in the middle of telling things. That was how she was.

By then I already thought of Meara as a kind of baseball—the kind Clyde was forever finding and bringing home with him. Under the torn white hide there'd be all this string, wound so tight you'd think it covered something at the center, but if you unraveled it to get the whole story, you'd just have a pile of string at the end and a tiny piece of cork. Not what you wanted. I lay back against the smooth face of the ledge, feeling quieter and quieter, thinking about hardballs and softballs and tennis balls—all sorts of balls that Clyde's chewed through. The pounding in my heart stopped after a while and I could feel how still the night was.

It was too much to think about. Usually, if I have too much to think about, I go and find Clyde and rest my head against him. Lying there, all I'll think about is the heave of his chest and the steady way he breathes when he's asleep.

The stars were very bright. I looked over at Meara. She looked happy. She was watching the stars with a smile on her face.

I thought back to what Ruby had said. Well, I can be happy, too, I thought. Just like Meara is happy. I can be happy about anything I learn.

The leaves rustled in the summer breeze and the crickets pulsed behind us. I thought back to the things I'd seen that day: the flower wreath, and Douglas finding Meara in the meadow; the look on Douglas's face, and the sunburn on his cheeks; those blond snarls at the back of his head that he never likes you to brush. How sweet the pasture smelled, and how Douglas's sweetness could fill up a whole room sometimes, like it had when he talked about the sand crabs. How I could just see the sand crabs—pale as thumbnails, digging away.

I took a deep breath. The ringing of the crickets was like thunder in my ears. I thought about how Ruby told me I was sweet right in the middle of my worst stubbornness, how the color of her ruby ring was the color of the strawberry she'd saved for me, and how much she loved to make me French coffee with sugar and hot milk. Then I thought about Mom pushing her saucer toward me so that I'd have a place to hide the hot milk skin, and remembering that, I loved my mom so much. I just lay there, loving the whole day, with a big lump of happiness in my throat.

CHAPTER TWENTY-TWO

I began to meet Meara by the pond a lot after that—almost every night. Sometimes Clyde would want to follow, but the one time I let him, he wouldn't settle down once we got back home, and he almost woke everybody up by panting and running back and forth from the hallway to the back door.

After the first time, I didn't always go in the pond because I couldn't stop the memory of how cold the water had been. Meara swam every night, though, so when I didn't go in, I'd sit on the ledge and watch her. Something about the way she gleamed out there

151

in the pond reminded me of a candle lighting up a dark window.

Sometimes I'd dive in, just to please her. She loved to play in the water, loved to pull herself underneath, where I hated to follow, so she could surface close to me, without warning. Afterward, we'd sit together on the rock ledge, and I'd be shivering and blowing on the tips of my fingers to warm them. So many times she'd giggle and say, "Oh, Molly, you're cold!" Each time she'd say it, it would be like she'd forgotten what I was like in the first place—that I got cold often, and she didn't, or couldn't.

During the daytime, we'd play in the meadow and make up stories. We used to dress up with clothes from Ruby's trunk. We'd make costumes for Douglas, too, and tie bright scarves around Clyde's neck.

We held races down the length of road to the bluff, and Clyde would win. At lunch, Mom made a huge bunch of sandwiches—peanut butter for Douglas. She'd let Meara squeeze the lemons for lemonade. Actually, I was in charge of the lemonade because Meara always made it too sweet. In the afternoons, we'd pick blackberries and raspberries and fill up our sand pails. When we'd empty them out, we'd see rivers of berry juice, all brilliant and purple against the yellow plastic.

Sometimes Ruby would make cobbler with the berries and we'd help. Later, after supper, we'd all meet over at her house. Mom and Dad would take over a big half-gallon of vanilla ice cream, and the mounds of ice cream and hot berry cobbler would melt together and make pink or lavender.

Pie days were my favorite. Pie days were the most fun because Ruby would let Meara or me help roll out the dough and make the fork marks at the end, like sparrow tracks. Toward the end of summer, she gave each of us our own little tart tin, and we each got to make our own berry tart. What she'd do with Douglas, besides letting him lick the filling bowls, was to let him sprinkle cinnamon-sugar over the leftover dough. Then she'd roll the strips into tiny logs and we'd bake them on a cookie sheet. The logs would be our treat with milk, when the pies were cooling. Meara thought the cinnamon idea was very good, because she always had this huge temptation to taste the pies right away.

By August, Clyde had developed this new trick that he practiced around tables. You'd be working on some dough or pouring sugar into a mixing bowl, and there would be Clyde, sitting up on his hind legs, swaying slightly and begging with his eyes. He could sit that way, absolutely silent, for a very long time. Sometimes I'd look over at him, and his eyes would be sort of glazed over as if he'd forgotten a long time ago why he was doing this. I'd always slip him something then, though with Clyde, it almost seemed worse to give him a little piece of treat because he'd remember it for hours. He'd plant himself in the exact same spot and sway there like a little pine tree.

We spent every spare moment down by the beach. Meara would wear a big straw sun hat of Ruby's so she wouldn't get too hot. That was great because I could always spot her hat from the top of the bluff.

I get really tan in the summer and my hair gets sun streaks in it. Meara stayed pale, though on some days the red starburst seemed brighter. It was just one of those things about Meara. I used to put my arm next to hers to compare, and the colors were like the clouds of milk Ruby'd pour into my coffee bowl mixing with the milky shade of the coffee.

Meara loved the ocean and she'd cheer for us when we raced the waves, but she never went in.

Douglas asked about it for a long time, because to him every day is new, like starting over. "Wanna swim?" he'd ask Meara, all set to laugh in case she said yes, because Douglas laughs when he's happy. But Meara wouldn't say yes to him, and when he didn't hear the word he wanted, he'd just stand there, disappointed. "But I want you to," he'd say, and Meara

would smile, as if he should know better than to keep
asking, and shake her head slowly from side to side.
That way, Douglas would laugh and hug her, forgetting
about how much sand he was covered with. We'd
shriek at him to get off our blanket and he would.
He'd run off to sit at the edge of the waves and put
handfuls of wet sand on his knees.

Douglas was the only one who kept asking,
though. Mom and Dad didn't. I guess they thought she
was scared of the water. I never thought to tell anyone
about our swims at night. Certainly not Douglas.

After all, it was almost true, what they all thought.
Except that she wasn't scared of water, she was scared
of *ocean*.

CHAPTER TWENTY-THREE

One morning the birds woke me up early, and once I'd opened my eyes to see the blue sky, I couldn't close them back up. Douglas and I had blueberries for breakfast and afterward went to get Meara to go to the beach. It was too hot for anything but swimsuits by ten o'clock.

I didn't notice it haze over at first because I was lying on my stomach, reading. But once the wind picked up, the backs of my legs began prickling with goose bumps. We were almost the only people left.

Douglas was playing nearby, digging in the sand with a Dixie cup. I called him to come and pack up.

We wriggled back into our cutoffs and tops and I laced up Douglas's sneakers. I thought he was going to cry for a second, because he likes to stay barefoot, but Meara whispered something to him and he brightened right up.

She lifted him up and placed him on her right hip and he dangled his legs.

"Are you going to carry him all the way up?" I asked in a grumpy way. "He's too heavy!" And to Douglas I said, "Douglas, you are too heavy," but Meara just smiled and said, "Not for me," the way she'd answered Ruby that time before. So I gave up. Now it was really bothering me that it would be cloudy.

Sometimes the climb up by the bluff makes your legs ache, even when you have nothing to carry. I could hear Meara counting the number of her steps in a singsong way so Douglas would count along with her: "five . . . six . . . seven. . . ." Then as her breath got shorter and Douglas trailed off (he can't count beyond twenty): ". . . twenty-two . . . twenty-three . . . twenty-four. . . ."

I was so far ahead of them, I stopped and crouched on a little rise to wait. The ocean was gray and the breakers had high white crests. When Meara caught up, her face was flushed. "Forty-two!" she called out. "Forty-two steps and only halfway up.

157

Forty-two steps for Douglas!" She grinned at me. Then she turned back to Douglas and asked, "So, forty-two steps for Douglas, and for who else? For who else, Douglas?" She laughed and hugged him to get a better grip before starting to climb. "For who else, Douglas?" I thought for sure he'd say *her* name.

"Love," said Douglas in a perfectly clear voice. I just looked at him and Meara looked at him, too. It was an odd word to come out of such a little boy. The way he said it, it had a capital letter. Meara was happy.

"You're right," she told him, and we climbed the rest of the way with Meara smiling, her breath growing heavier, and Douglas looking like he was seeing the world from the top of an elephant.

CHAPTER TWENTY-FOUR

We went straight to Ruby's. Large drops of rain began to fall, spotting the dirt road. It was a chill rain, but there wasn't enough of it to soak us. When Ruby opened the door, Meara set Douglas down. He traipsed into the sitting room and sat down by himself in front of the fire, politely. I took my shoes off to dry my toes while Meara curled against the front of the couch. The firelight gave everything in the room a hint of amber, like an old photograph.

The storm broke then, as if someone had turned a bowl over and spilled the rain out on the roof. The windows were almost solid sheets of water. We sat quietly. I could hear Ruby in the kitchen: the clang of pots, then silence, then the sound of popcorn crackling in the pan.

"Oh, good," I said, "popcorn." Douglas smiled but he didn't take his eyes off the fire. The popping was as loud as the rain on the roof and there was the perfect smell of melting butter. When it was done, Ruby brought it in for us in a huge bread bowl and placed the bowl in the middle of the rug. Ruby sat in a rocker, though, not on the floor with us. She scooped out a handful of the popcorn for herself and kept it on a napkin in her lap, eating one piece at a time.

I could hardly believe she was the same person as that girl in the photograph.

"Tell us a story," I said.

"A happy one or a sad one?"

"Happy," said Meara.

"Happy or sad," I said, nudging her with my foot. You couldn't be too picky around Ruby.

"Would you like to hear the story of The Blue Dress?" asked Ruby, and everyone nodded. She began to creak back and forth in the rocker. Her fingers folded and unfolded the napkin into little squares and back out flat again as she talked.

"Once upon a time," Ruby said, "when I was very young, it was my habit to walk past the General

Store on my way back from school. During the winter months, old Mr. Thomas would turn on his window lamp at dusk—"

"Was that Clarence's father?" I asked, and she nodded.

"I knew that," I whispered to Meara.

"Things might look a little drab in the front window by daylight, but by the light of that little lamp, everything on display looked enchanted, even the steam iron and the bolts of flannel. After several weeks of looking, I heard a tapping at the window. Mr. Thomas had noticed me out there in my coat and muffler and motioned me in. In I went and I looked around.

"The store had a pleasant smell to it, like fruit-cake. There was an old potbellied stove that heated the place, and Mr. Thomas drew me up a chair close by it, and one for himself. I was about to sit when he asked if I'd like to pick a candy stick from one of the jars on the counter. Of course, I said yes—"

"Of course," I said, hugging my knees.

"I stood there awhile, trying to decide which color I wanted. Which do you think I picked?" asked Ruby.

"Grape," Douglas said, completely engrossed.

"You're absolutely right, Douglas," Ruby said. "I picked out a grape swirl and then I went and sat

161

down while Mr. Thomas waited on some customers. By the time he finished, I had the top of the grape stick whittled to a point and I had to be careful not to hurt my tongue.

"Mr. Thomas sat down opposite me and lit his pipe. I liked him, I remember. I felt very proud to have been invited in, even though the smell of the pipe tobacco made my head ache. Mr. Thomas opened the door of the potbellied stove to throw more heat in the room, and when he did, I began to look around the store. That's when I saw it—"

"Saw what?" Meara asked.

"The Blue Dress," Ruby said, smiling.

"What?" Douglas said.

"Blue," I told him, "blue dress."

"Blue," he repeated, as though blue were a kind of flavor, like grape.

Ruby spoke in a sort of hush: "It hung on some sort of clotheshorse with wrought-iron legs. The dress was a bright gentian blue, made all out of satin, with tiny cap sleeves and a small waist. And," Ruby whispered, "there was a blue rose sewn in at the bodice, of matching satin." Ruby paused and looked at us, one by one. "A beautiful dress," she said.

"Mr. Thomas saw me staring at the dress and he laughed and said that he wished he was a painter and could paint my picture, just like that. 'You've never seen the dress before?' he asked. I shook my head. He chuckled. 'Makes you want to dance, doesn't it?' I nodded, though I didn't know anything about dancing. 'Here now,' Mr. Thomas said, "would you like to try it on?' So I told him yes, without wasting a word, and I whisked myself into the back room and put the dress on without a mirror and as quickly as I could because the back room was very cold. It was much too long for me. The waist gapped and it was too full on top, but it was so very beautiful. The satin skirt made the faintest rustle, and close up, the dress was bluer than anything I could have imagined—bluer than summer."

"Bluer than the sky?" I asked.

Ruby smiled. "Bluer than the sky."

"Bluer than the ocean?" Meara asked suddenly.

"Bluer than the ocean," Ruby said.

She went on: "I walked over to the mirror by the yard goods and stood on tiptoe and turned around slowly. 'Don't drag the hem,' Mr. Thomas said. Then he picked me up and set me on a stool. The skirt draped gracefully and didn't quite reach the floor."

"It must have been beautiful," Meara whispered.

"Then," Ruby said, "Mr. Thomas taught me the waltz—it's a kind of dance. Mr. Thomas set his pipe down and held one of my hands out to the side and placed my other hand on his shoulder. Then he sort of rolled the little stool around the room with me standing on it so I could get the feel of dancing. He hummed the music, and at the end, he gave me a little bow and told me that if the dress was still there when I grew up, I could have it.

"And that very Christmas, it lay under my tree, though I didn't know till I opened the package. Mr. Thomas had wrapped it for me himself, with a little note that said he hoped all my dreams would come true as easily."

I clapped my hands with relief. That started Douglas clapping.

"Where is it?" Meara asked. "I want to see." So Ruby got up and went to her closet. We could hear her rummaging. She came back holding the blue dress and it was every bit as beautiful as she'd said.

Meara got up to stroke the material, and laid her cheek against the soft folds. I held Douglas back so he wouldn't get it all full of popcorn butter.

"Such blue," Meara said softly. Then she let go of the dress and looked up at Ruby.

"But not bluer than the ocean," she said. A look passed between them then. Ruby reached down and

164

smoothed the wisps of dark hair away from Meara's eyes.

"Is that the end of the story?" I asked.

Ruby shook her head. She hung the dress on the back of the door and took Douglas onto her lap. It was close to naptime for him, and every so often his eyes would flutter closed.

"The rest is a love story," said Ruby. "Are you sure you want to hear it?"

"Oh, yes," I whispered.

"I fell in love only once," said Ruby, "and his name was Jimmy Blaine. He was the best dancer on the island, and all the girls were crazy for him. He gave me this ring," she said, showing us.

"And the lamp—" I interrupted. "Did he give you the mermaid lamp?"

Ruby nodded. "We picked it out together," she said. "He wanted to leave me something to wish on, for good luck, because he'd enlisted to fight overseas, and we both knew what that could mean." She paused.

"No love without danger," she said softly, looking right at me so I'd remember. Then she spoke again, even more sadly: "Ask anyone who loves the ocean."

"So true," Meara whispered, and it gave me a lump in my throat.

"Mom said he never came home," I said.

"No"—Ruby sighed—"he didn't.

"Jimmy had a month's leave. We were so excited, we decided we'd get married that very month. He'd written me to meet his ferry, and to wear the blue dress, rain or shine. But he didn't come on the evening ferry, nor on the late ferry, and I couldn't understand it. Finally I walked over to his mother's house, near the landing. The curtains were drawn and I wasn't sure anyone was home, but she came to the door, finally. That was when she told me that Jimmy'd been killed. There'd been a telegram—"

"How did he die?" I asked, even though I knew you weren't supposed to.

"He drowned," she said, and her voice was far away. "His ship hit a mine."

"What did you do when she told you?" I asked.

Ruby smoothed Douglas's curls. "I walked," she said. "I walked all the way home from Gilbert's Landing. After the first mile, I took off my shoes. I threw them away when I got tired of them. After the second or third mile, I limped badly, but I wanted it that way. I wanted the pain in my feet to match the pain in my heart. I walked my feet raw—"

"Like the belly of your little seal," I whispered.

166

"Yes"—Ruby smiled sadly —"and still my heart ached."

Douglas sighed and turned in his sleep. Ruby began to hum softly and rock him.

"What song is that?" I asked, though I knew.

"The seal song," she answered. "I learned it that night. Would you like to hear how?"

We both nodded. Meara's eyes filled with tears.

"I kept walking," she continued, "and the moon rose, and the stars rose, and still I walked and walked. I thought I would never stop walking. In the waves out by our own beach, I heard the song. I couldn't see at first who was singing, and to this day, I'm not sure. I was so weak and heartsore, and I'd been crying so long. But I thought it was a seal—"

"The Great Bull Seal," I whispered.

"Yes"—she nodded—"only, somehow I understood his words, and the voice that sang to me was a kind voice. I didn't know what to think. I didn't think anything but a seal could swim in such cold waters, but then again, I didn't think seals could sing.

"In the moonlight, as I watched him, he took a different shape—"

"What do you mean?" I asked.

"Well, his face seemed to grow longer, more like

167

the face of a man. As I watched, he pulled himself out of the water, onto the rocks. I was exhausted, I admit, but even in that darkness, I saw clearly, and I grew frightened, because he seemed a man and not a seal at all.

"I must have fallen asleep. I woke near the rocks the next morning, and I can't be sure for certain it wasn't all a dream. But to this day I could swear that seal spoke to me—dream or no. He said he was sorry to hear me mourn. He said he knew what it was to mourn, and that the sea was a better grave than some got, but still a sad place—for one as beloved as my Jimmy. 'How could you know,' I asked, and he said the sea kept no secrets from him, for he knew her language, and I should take comfort because he'd always be watching. Always. Never far from the shore of my heart."

"And he told me to love again"—Ruby smiled—"because that's what the waves say."

"And did you?" I asked, holding my breath.

"Of course," she said, "don't I love you?"

"But it's not true," I said, letting my breath out all at once. "The waves don't say that. They don't say anything."

"Oh yes, they do," Ruby said softly. "The waves say to love again, no matter what."

168

CHAPTER TWENTY-FIVE

C H A P T E R   TWENTY-FIVE

By then the storm was over and patches of blue sky broke through the clouds. The road back to our house had big puddles in the wheel ruts, so I carried Douglas. He was still happy but very sleepy, and he leaned his head on my shoulder. Mom took one look at him when I walked in and said, "Naptime."

I got him out of his clothes and into his pajamas. Then I took him into the bathroom and scrubbed the butter off his face with a washcloth and soaped his hands under the faucet. He was very quiet the whole time, which is unusual for Douglas. When I laid him down, he didn't grumble or ask for a drink of water.

169

I stretched out on my bed, opposite him. He watched me for a little while. Every so often, his eyelids would close, then he'd open them back up again.

"Aren't you sleepy?" I asked.

"No," he said.

"Didn't you like the story?"

He nodded. I wished him sweet dreams and I got up to pull the shade down. He wanted to know where I was going, so I told him I was going to read my book.

"But where are you *going?*" he asked again, and the last word sort of screeched out so that I wouldn't leave.

"Just in the other room," I told him. I sat down next to him and started rubbing his back some. "Pretend it's nighttime," I said. " 'Night, Douglas."

" 'Night," he said in a muffled voice.

I started naming the things in his room: "Good night, bed."

"Good night," he echoed.

"Good night, bookcase."

" 'Night, BOOKCASE," he shouted, triumphant.

"Don't shout like that," I told him. I let the room get all quiet again so that he'd get the idea of the game better.

"Good night, books," I said.

170

" 'Night, books," he said happily.

"Good night, truck."

" 'Night," he repeated.

"Good night, sneakers," I said.

" 'Night, SNEAKERS," he said, and he looked like he was going to sit up and shout again.

"No shouting, Douglas," I warned. I tried to think of more things to name. "Good night, blueberries," I said. "Good night, popcorn," and he'd echo right after me. "Good night, ocean," I said. He looked right at me as though that was the biggest joke in the world and started laughing.

Then he wanted to pick out the names himself and make me say them.

"FISHES," he'd say, and I'd say obediently: "Good night, fishes."

"WAVES," he said, and I told the waves good night.

"BOATS," he said, and I told the boats good night.

"SELZ," he said.

"Good night, selz," I said, and then to show it was the end: "Good night, Douglas."

He lay very still with a little smile on his face, and then he put his arms up to give me a kiss.

171

"Douglas," I said, tucking the blankets in around him, "what are selz?"

"Selz," he said, and again, very plainly, "selz." I wished Mom were there because she always understands what he's trying to say.

"What is it?" I asked. "A bird?" He shook his head. "A fish?" I asked. He shook his head again, gleaming with excitement that I couldn't guess.

"Selz," he said, and he held his head way up out of the covers, trying to make me understand. "In the ocean," he said.

"Seals!" I exclaimed, giggling. "You mean seals, Douglas."

"Yes." He nodded happily and said the word again. "Selz."

Then, out of the blue he said, "Like *Mer*." Mer was his name for Meara.

"Oh, Douglas," I said, "what are you saying?" I sort of jiggled the bed to make him laugh, because I didn't like this at all.

"Meara's not a seal," I told him firmly, but he just looked at me without budging.

"Mer's not a seal"—I tried his name for her— "she's a girl."

He didn't say anything. I tried to smile.

172

"She looks like a girl, doesn't she?" I asked, and he nodded.

"Well, you can't be both," I told him. "Douglas, who said Meara was a seal?"

"She did," he said, and he closed his eyes, happily, with a sleepy sigh.

CHAPTER TWENTY-SIX

C H A P T E R   TWENTY-SIX

I didn't have anything to say to that, so I left the room
and headed for the back door. "Come on, Clyde," I
yelled, and I stormed out, banging the screen. There
were patches of blue sky but still some clouds.

I walked straight over to Ruby's and knocked
loudly. "Where's Meara?" I demanded. I had to shade
my eyes to look at her.

"Down at the seashore," Ruby said. She paused,
holding the door open. "Are you coming in?"

I was already on my way. I called over my shoulder, "If you see her, you tell her I'm looking for her."

I said it the way my dad says it when he means some-one's in trouble.

I ran all the way down to the shore. Clyde was way ahead of me. I took big hopping leaps down the bluff and slipped in places. I was out of breath when I reached the bottom, and my sneakers were full of sand. Clyde was running along the edge of the water.

"Meara!" I shouted. I could see her, farther down the flat stretch. I called her name again and she turned and waved. I didn't care what she was doing or if she was happy. I was furious. I took big angry steps across the beach and the way my feet sank in the sand just made everything worse. I kept marching. Finally I stood in front of her, breathing hard. I couldn't think how to begin—I just glared.

"What do you mean telling Douglas you're a seal—"

She didn't answer.

"Meara!" I was trembling. "What do you mean, telling Douglas? What do you mean telling him some-thing like that?"

I started to cry. "I don't care if you're a seal," I said, accusing her with every bone in my body. "I don't care what you are."

175

She held herself absolutely still and just stared at me.

"I don't care what you are," I repeated, "but you shouldn't have told Douglas like that. It's not fair!" I stamped at her. "I loved you first," I said. "You're my friend. You should have told me." Clyde came running up then, with his tail wagging away, slapping at my knees. I took both my hands and gave him a huge push away from me. He yelped with fear because I'd thrown him off balance, and then he just lay where I'd shoved him. There was sand on his face and he was shivering. I wanted to run to him and hug his neck, but I couldn't stop crying, and I couldn't move.

"I loved you first, Meara," I said. "Why didn't you tell me?" I stood there, and the sobs made my chest jerk.

Clyde didn't move from where he lay; he just watched. I sat down in a heap and buried my face in my arms. I felt Meara put her hand on my shoulder, but I shrugged it off.

"Just leave me alone," I said. We sat there for a while in silence. She put her hand back on my shoulder and I felt it make a cool shadow. I knew it must be hurting her to be out in the sun. She'd forgotten her hat.

"Molly," she whispered finally, "Moll—" And

she took my face in her hands and laid her cheek against mine the same way she'd done with Ruby's dress. "Oh, Moll, how sad you are. I'm so sorry. I'm so sorry," she repeated.

Clyde started to inch forward toward us on his belly, but I gave him a horrible look, so he stopped.

"Why did you tell Douglas?" I asked.

"Oh, Molly." She sighed and rubbed her face against mine, so both our faces were wet and salty with tears. "Not to hurt you," she said. "We were playing here one day and we saw seals lift their heads out of the bay to look at us. Douglas laughed and pointed and asked what they were. I told him they were seals, those funny little heads in the water. Then"—she hesitated—"I don't know why, but I told him that I was one, too."

"Is it true?"

Meara nodded. I thought for a minute.

"Does Ruby know?" I asked. "Did you tell her?"

Meara shook her head. "No. She just knows. Ruby found me on the shore path. I couldn't talk, I was shivering so badly. She never asked me anything, but I think when you . . ." Her voice fell off. ". . . when I first met you and you told about the dead seal—" She raised her eyes to mine and I saw such pain in them. "I think Ruby understood then."

177

"Understood what?" I asked. There was a great roaring in my ears, against what I would hear, like surf rolling me over and over. I tried not to think of the bloodstains on the snow.

Meara stared at me for a long time. She tightened her grip on my hand.

"She was my mother," she whispered. Her eyes filled with tears.

"But how—"

"Some of us can change. We can look just like you. We can stay forever, if we want." She swallowed with an effort. "It takes salt water to change us back."

I stared at her, not believing. She looked the same as she always did.

"It was my fault," Meara whispered. "We were swimming close to shore, too close." Clyde started to make a high whining sound because he was so miserable.

"But why?"

"I just wanted to visit," she said in that same hushed voice. She tightened her grip on my hand.

"To visit," she repeated, with her eyes on the sea. "To walk and run and skip and play—to climb trees, run down hills, wade through flowers. To look down and see hands and fingers and wrists; to hold a spoon, turn a page, stroke your hair." She looked at

178

me and the tears rolled down her face. "To touch you," she said, and she brought her other hand up and laid it against my cheek.

"And the sounds, Molly, that would reach us from the shore—I used to dream about them. I'd heard wonderful stories about those who'd gone ashore and returned. How I wanted to talk, just for a little while, and to laugh and shout and—" She swallowed. "And I wanted to meet you. Not *you*, Molly—I mean, I didn't know you—but I wanted you to be here, all the same."

Clyde gave up and laid his head on his front paws.

I gave her hand a little squeeze. Her whole body was trembling with the effort to speak.

"My mother understood—about wanting something the way I did—and she knew it would just be for a little while, for a visit, that when I tired of arms and legs, I'd come home." Clyde whined again, low in his throat. "But everything went wrong—

"I was caught fast in the net, no matter which way I twisted. My mother circled back for me and tore the netting so I could get away, but she was hauled up herself before she could swim free. And though I followed the boat to shore, I was too little to save her. So I hid in the rocks and tried not to listen to the drunken voices or the sounds of the knife."

"Oh, Meara," I whispered, "it's too horrible—"

179

She nodded and the tears rolled down her face. "But you came and sang to me," she said.

"Sang to you?"

"You *called* for me to come. You called, and your call came when I had no one, and something happened. Something happened to loosen the grip of the ocean on me—"

We sat there quietly. The tide began to creep toward us. The sky was pure blue now and there was quite a bit of surf.

"Do you miss it?" I asked after a while. "Do you miss the ocean?"

"Sometimes."

I nodded.

"I miss my mother," she said softly. "And I'll always miss her—but, oh, Molly, I have *you*," and she looked at me with such love it was like a wave breaking over me. "You're my family now, you and Ruby." She would have gone on, but she stopped to wait for me, the way you do when you're wading in and you don't want the waves to hit your stomach without the other person there. I started to laugh then. I felt the way I used to feel when my dad would throw me up in the air above his head and catch me in his arms.

"I know," I said, and she was laughing, too. "It's

180

you and me and Ruby and *Douglas*." With each name
I said, she said yes, and I thought we would float away
then, each name was so full of love. I thought we'd
be carried off by love, like helium balloons get carried
off when no one holds on. "You and me and Ruby and
Douglas and *Clyde*," and I shouted out *Clyde*, so of
course, he was there in a second; and the tears melted
all out of my eyes and I stroked him and Meara stroked
him, and he turned and kept turning in circles so we
wouldn't run out of hands for him. I said over and over
how good a dog he was and how sorry I was I pushed
him down.

We fell down on the sand to catch our breath and
Clyde picked his way in and out of our arms and legs,
trying to lick our faces. You're totally defenseless with
him when you're on your back.

"Quick, roll over!" I said, so we rolled over on
our stomachs and Clyde charged off down the beach
after some sea gulls.

The sun was like a warm hand on the back of my
head. I squinted out at the waves. My question drifted
back to me like a little wisp of cloud.

"But still, Meara," I asked, "don't you miss the
ocean?"

"I have the ocean," she said, like it was a jar of
pennies she'd been saving forever.

"No." I shook my head. "I mean to swim in it— the way you used to." It was sort of a lame question, but I didn't know how else to ask it.

She shook her head. "Besides, I can't ever go back—not just to swim. Once I do, it's forever."

"But if it's your home—"

"No," she said softly. She tucked her hand back in mine and we lay there some, watching the sunlight sparkle on the water. Then some eagerness came back in her fingers and she gripped my hand tightly.

"Moll . . . so blue though, for miles and miles, no edge, no shore . . ." She sighed wistfully and grinned and laid her head down in the crook of her arm. A warm breeze lifted the edges of her dress. I wondered if Ruby would make one for me if I asked; she made such nice shifts for Meara.

Clyde came back to us, dripping with salt water. He dropped a short piece of driftwood in front of me so I could reach it, and then he backed off, barking, so he could get as much of a head start as possible. I got up and threw the stick for him as far as I could— out past the breakers. He was gone in a flash.

I had to know for sure. "Meara, you're not going back, are you?"

She looked right at me.

"No," she said, "of course not."

"No?" I squeaked, joyfully.

"No!" she said. Her eyes were as blue as the ocean. I made her say it about ten more times. Clyde brought the stick back, panting, and the water ran off his sides in little rivers.

"Watch out, he'll shake," I said, and Meara shouted at him not to. Then I picked up the stick and threw it even farther than I had before. I was so happy.

CHAPTER   TWENTY-SEVEN
C H A P T E R   TWENTY-SEVEN

I heard Mom calling my name. She was carrying Douglas down the bluff. I waved and she waved back. By then Clyde was back with his stick and he flopped to the sand about ten feet from us, panting like a sturdy black engine.

"What time do you think it is?" I asked Meara.

"I don't know," she answered, and looked up at the sun, "maybe four o'clock?"

"I'm hungry," I said. "Maybe you can come for supper later."

"Maybe," she said, and we smiled at each other.

Mom set Douglas down and straightened up with

184

her hand on her back. "You're getting so big, Douglas!" she said, and Douglas nodded to show he'd thought up the whole idea himself. "I'm going to leave him here with you two." She bent over to hike his swimming trunks higher up around his waist. "Come back in an hour or so, we'll eat early," Mom said. "You can help with the green beans," she called over her shoulder. Clyde trotted along with Mom as far as the bluff, but he came running back when I whistled.

"I love green beans." Meara giggled.

"Good," I said, "you can help. She means we have to fix them."

I stood up and stripped to my bathing suit. I still had it on from the morning. Clyde had to bring me the stick again, so I gave it a long heave and off he went, bounding through the water.

"I'm going in," I announced. "You'll watch Douglas?"

"Of course," Meara said, and she made a big hoop of her arms and pulled him backward onto her lap.

I took some slow leaping steps forward, then I gave up and dove under a wave. I couldn't believe the water could be so cold with the sun so hot. I swam out over my head and then turned back and waved at the shore. Meara and Douglas waved back.

185

Out beyond the breakers, it was so peaceful. I floated on my back for a while, squinting up at the sun every so often. My face would begin to get dry and hot, then I'd dive under again and swim some more. Meara and Douglas looked like little dots on the beach.

I could lie out here forever, I thought. The water lapped gently at my ears and the sun glittered on the waves. It was like being rocked in a cradle.

Just then, something dragged my arm under. I floundered momentarily and came up coughing and sputtering. It was Clyde.

"Clyde, what are you doing here!" I was treading water. He still had the stick in his mouth, which made it hard for him to breathe. He kept circling around me as if he was lost, and I could tell he was scared.

"Clyde," I called softly. "Good dog, come here," which was stupid because we were way too far out, but I wanted to do something to stop Clyde from breathing in that horrible choked way.

He veered toward me, breaking the circle, but when I tried to grab him, one of his back legs raked my thigh. He started to whimper through his raspy breathing.

"Drop the stick, Clyde," I whispered, but he wouldn't drop it. He was very frightened.

186

My leg hurt. I wondered if it was bleeding. I was scared to be out there in the water, bleeding. "Good dog," I whispered. "It's okay, it'll be okay." I think I was crying. "Good puppy, sweet puppy," I whispered. I tried to get him to look at me so he would follow me in toward the shore, but he kept going in these crazy circles, as if nine people were calling him at once.

My breath was coming in gasps. "C'mon, puppy," I said, "this way," but he started thrashing. He can't see me, I thought, and I swam toward him and grabbed the back of his neck. He struggled in my hands and twisted and we both went under. I got so mixed up, I didn't know which way to swim; so I opened my eyes underwater and even though I saw it coming, Clyde kicked me again—his nails raking me across the flat of my stomach.

I didn't have enough breath left to talk to him. Please don't let my puppy drown, I prayed. Don't let him drown. He still had the stick in his mouth. I tried for it and it made some spark come back to him, but he lunged away to keep hold of it. My leg hurt and I tried not to kick so I could rest some, but my arms weren't strong enough and I swallowed seawater. I went under again and with my eyes open underwater, I could see the red blood curling out of the slashes on my leg

187

and stomach. A scream rose in my throat and I clawed for the surface. I couldn't see Clyde or anything. My hair was matted across my face and I couldn't breathe. I groped blindly in front of me. I thought I felt him then, felt his sweet round head and shoulders, so I threw my arms around him and hugged him. I couldn't bear to let go, and then, somehow, we broke the surface and I gasped for air. I choked and coughed, and when I got my breath, I just clung to his neck, sobbing.

When I could, I lifted up my head to see where we were. But it wasn't Clyde I held. It was a small gray seal. I twisted my head to find Clyde and I could see him ahead of us, pointed toward shore. We'd nose him along whenever he started to circle off course. I was so tired, I just pressed my face against the neck of the seal and watched Clyde's head as we moved through the water, getting closer and closer to the beach.

I could see Douglas running along the sand. I tried to lift my arm up to wave at him, but I was too weak. By the time we were in far enough for me to stand, Clyde was just barely making it. His breath rattled like a broken part, so I let go of the seal. I splashed toward him and gathered him up in my arms and rocked him. "It's okay, puppy, it's okay," I said, and I half-carried, half-guided him in to shore.

He was so heavy out of water that I stumbled and dropped to my knees alongside of him. We lay there in about an inch of water. "Oh, Clyde, please be okay," I begged, and I heard his tail splash feebly as he licked at my tears.

Douglas piled on top of us then, so it was all three of us in a heap, and we hugged and kissed and rocked together. Douglas had been crying, too, so I said his name over and over to calm him. The places I'd been clawed were still welling with blood.

"It's okay," I told Douglas so he wouldn't be afraid. "It's from Clyde's toenails. We'll have to clip them later." Douglas drew back a little. "He didn't mean to," I said. "See, he just needs a kiss," and I bent and kissed Clyde's head, so Douglas did, too.

"Where's Meara?" I asked.

Douglas just pointed. I didn't understand, because he was pointing at the ocean.

Then my whole body went cold.

"Oh, no," I said. "No!" I shouted it, and I saw Meara, like in my dream, pushing against the window with all her might, and the window breaking anyway. I started running back into the water. Every step hurt. "Douglas, you stay with Clyde!" I yelled, "Don't move!" and I kept running. I called out Meara's name as I ran.

She came up from beneath the waves when the water was chest-high. She was just a little seal, gray, with a small gray face, but her eyes were blue and I knew her, and I knew what she'd just done for us.

"Meara," I said softly, knowing that she couldn't answer. She nosed up to me and nipped at my fingers gently. Her eyes were so blue. So blue. "Oh, Meara," I said, and stared at her. I put my hand out to her face and it was slick and silky, like an inner tube. I laid my head against her neck and hugged for dear life for the second time that day until I felt us breathing in rhythm. Each breath tore another strip from my heart. Like birch bark, I thought. Oh, good-bye, my friend. Good-bye, my darling friend.

I don't know how long it was. After a while she nudged me toward shore. I whistled for Clyde and gathered up my clothes slowly, wrapping my shirt around my leg where the cut was deepest. Then I lifted Douglas in my arms and we climbed the bluff home.

CHAPTER TWENTY-EIGHT

They found her white dress the next day, caught against the rocks of the seawall. When they asked me, I said I didn't know, I hadn't seen her. When they asked Douglas, he'd get very excited and point toward the water where she'd disappeared. Where did she go? they'd ask him. So he'd tell them: the ocean. But it was the wrong question. They never thought to ask him what she was.

No one scolded Clyde. Mom washed the welts on my stomach and dressed the cut on my leg with iodine. She sponged me and helped me into my nightgown. She put me into bed and brought my supper to me on a tray, but I couldn't eat. I was still shivering. Every so often I'd reach down over the side of the bed to pet Clyde's head.

Two or three days passed like that. I stayed in bed most of the time. Ruby would stop by and bring me puddings and things, but we didn't talk much. On the third day, I heard her tell Mom and Dad that she didn't think Meara had drowned. Someone closed a door so I wouldn't hear, but I heard anyway.

Ruby said that she'd suspected, from the first, that Meara had just run away, and last night she'd heard from her niece that Meara was back with them, safe. Mom murmured how glad she was, and that I would be so pleased.

The bedroom door creaked open. Ruby came over and sat down on my bed.

"Hello, goatgirl," she said. She pulled the sheet aside to check the cut on my leg. "Healing nicely," she said. "How does it feel?"

"Hurts," I said.

"I know it does," she said softly. "I know it does."

"You lied to them just now," I said. "I heard you."

Ruby just smiled down at me, a little sadly, I thought.

"What should I have told them?" she asked.

"Well, for one thing, Meara didn't run away." I was furious. "She said you *knew*."

Ruby sighed. "Some things," she said, "I knew some things." She began to stroke my hair. She didn't stop at the tangles; she just smoothed her palm down the whole side of the curls she could reach.

"Once upon a time," she told me, "there was a pale green mermaid with lovely long arms. She'd wave her arms from her perch on the great reef, but the seas were dangerous and lured many strangers. Their boats would tear apart on the hidden reefs before they could reach her, and many lives were lost.

"The mermaid wept to cause such sorrow, and for many months she hid herself from view and ventured out only by moonlight, though it had once been her great happiness to sit in the glittering sun and comb her hair and scan the waves for sails. But it was too late." Ruby paused to look into my eyes. "By then, tales of her beauty had spread far and wide. The strangers came in their ships and passed too close for a glimpse of her. One by one, they drowned."

As she spoke, the tears slid, one by one, down the sides of my face and trickled into my ears.

"One night," Ruby said, "as she sat beneath the moon, a great schooner appeared with billowed sails. She thought her heart would break to see it sink. So she reached her arms up and with all her heart begged the moon to dip for her, and bit by bit, the moon dipped lower, till at last she held it high in her arms, and it shone like a beacon in the captain's eyes, and he turned the wheel, and the ship was saved."

"It's the story of the mermaid lamp," I whispered.

"Yes," she said.

"Did she die?" I asked. "Did the mermaid die when she held the moon?"

"I don't know," Ruby said.

"Say she didn't die," I begged her. "Say she didn't—"

"She didn't die," said Ruby softly.

"That's how Meara looked," I said. "That's how she looked that first night out on the bluff, holding her arms up to the moon. Meara would have done the same as that mermaid. Meara would have saved that ship—"

"You're right," said Ruby, "but instead she saved you." She smoothed my forehead. "And we're so glad she did. And you would have done the same for her."

"I don't care," I said.

"You're very lucky," she said. "You and Clyde could have drowned. You both could have drowned."

"But now Meara's *gone*."

"Hush," said Ruby softly. "The mermaid didn't

195

die when she held the moon, and Meara didn't die
when she saved you. It's just that she's gone away,
and it's a big place, the ocean."

"But now I don't have her anymore, and I'll never
see her again, not the way she was." I was sobbing.
"And she doesn't have us anymore, either. Oh, *please,*
say she has the moon as her friend now, forever. Please
say she's happy," I begged, "with the waves to play
in and the whole ocean back; I want her to be happy.
I'm afraid she'll miss us too much, *all of us,*" and I
threw myself at Ruby and she held me and rocked me.

Clyde padded in softly. I felt his cold nose nudging my arm. Douglas was there, too. I smelled his
clean hair and felt the bed shift as Ruby lifted him
onto the circle of her lap.

POSTSCRIPT
POSTSCRIPT

That was almost a year ago. It happened at the end of last summer, and this is the beginning of a new summer now. Each year, more and more people come to Ambrose, and we hardly ever see seals, and none with blue eyes.

Some flowers bloom every spring, and some skip a year. *Biennials* skip a year. Ruby says some kinds of cactus only bloom in December. And sometimes they don't bloom at all, especially if someone has placed them inside to watch for the flower in time for Christmas. I like the idea of the cactus sealing itself

197

up and not coming back to blossom until it's ready, no matter who's waiting.

Ruby says she thinks we'll see Meara again, though, if we're patient. She says she'll buy me a Christmas cactus so I can learn how to wait.

But what Ruby doesn't know is that it's different now. It's different than it was right after I said good-bye. Sometimes it makes me sad to remember, but not always. Sometimes I'll walk down to the shore when the sun is setting and there's no one there but me. I'll look out at the ocean, with all its pinks and purples shimmering, and her name will start pounding like a great bell in my chest. And sometimes when I'm swimming, and I get scared of how dark the ocean is, I remember how she called it blue. The most beautiful blue.

AUTHOR'S NOTE

From the coasts of Scotland and northern New England come legends of seals who live among us, in human form. They are called *selkies*, these people of the sea. While they are here, they do not tell what they are. The stories come later: the white seal maid whose hands are always colder than the hands of ordinary women; the great gray selkie whose purse bulges with sunken gold.

The process of transformation, itself, is mysterious. In some versions, grown selkies appear on moonlit rocks, where they shed their sealskins to sing and dance. Such a selkie can be captured, if her sealskin is captured. But she must be guarded always, and the briny skin locked away in a trunk. For a selkie wife, stolen from the sea, may at any moment steal back her skin and be off. To restore her seal shape, she has only to drape that sealskin back over her shoulders.

What I have done in *Seal Child* is to suggest a different manner of transformation. In my variant, selkies make their first change at will. To return, they have only to dive back into seawater. Such transformation is simpler but absolute. Those who choose it remain seals forever. The choice is theirs.